A total disaster...

I leaned back against the lockers, feeling sick. *I* was the one who'd started this—who'd screamed out the secret I had sworn I wouldn't tell.

Out of the corner of my eye I could see Damon still standing there. He'd seen the whole thing and was probably more convinced than ever that I was Ronald's girlfriend, or a nutcase, or just the meanest girl at SVJH.

Blindly I broke into a run, heading for the safety of the girls' room and wishing I could run away forever.

I'd ruined Ronald's life and lost all hope of ever going out with Damon—all before first period.

Don't miss any of the books in SWEET VALLEY JUNIOR HIGH, an exciting new series from Bantam Books!

Too
Popular

Written by
Jamie Suzanne

Created by
FRANCINE PASCAL

BANTAM BOOKS
NEW YORK•TORONTO•LONDON•SYDNEY•AUCKLAND

RL 4, 008-012

TOO POPULAR
A Bantam Book / October 1999

*Sweet Valley Junior High is a trademark of
Francine Pascal.*

Conceived by Francine Pascal.

*Produced by 17th Street Productions,
a division of Daniel Weiss Associates, Inc.
33 West 17th Street, New York, NY 10011.*

ISBN: 0-553-48667-5

Published simultaneously in the United States and Canada

*Bantam Books are published by Bantam Books, a division of Random
House, Inc. Its trademark, consisting of the words "Bantam Books" and
the portrayal of a rooster, is Registered in the U.S. Patent and Trademark
Office and in other countries. Marca Registrada. Bantam Books, 1540
Broadway, New York, New York 10036.*

PRINTED IN THE UNITED STATES OF AMERICA

OPM   0 9 8 7 6 5 4 3 2 1

To Nick Sanitsky

Jessica

1. Write a blank-verse poem on a topic that inspires and challenges you. Choose a subject that truly captures your imagination and mystifies you, and use the poem to pose a question to yourself.

~~Bad Hair Days~~
~~What is it that causes those mornings when nothing you do can make your hair look normal?~~

I told Mrs. Pomfrey that she had the wrong Wakefield twin. Elizabeth is the one with the writing genes. But then she got all technical and said that since we're identical twins, we have the same genes. I had to bite my tongue to keep from telling her that she teaches English, not biology.

So now I have to write some stupid poem about something that "mystifies" me. How about why I can't say anything around Damon Ross without making a major fool of myself? Every time I get near those gorgeous blue eyes, I turn into a total idiot. I'm talking major, fall-on-your-butt-in-spaghetti-sauce-and-burst-into-tears disasters. And I'm not exaggerating.

Anyway, I might as well vent my feelings on paper. No one's going to read it anyway.

<u>Silent Love</u>

Your smile melts my heart,
Your voice makes it pound.
But when I open my mouth, I can't
make a sound.
How can I show you how I feel?
Why won't you show me if you know?

Damon

Reasons to try to ask Jessica Wakefield out again, even though the last time I failed miserably:

1. "Do or do not. There is no try."
2. I can't stop thinking about her.
3. I can't even think about trying to stop thinking about her.
4. She might say yes.

Jessica

I've almost made it, I thought in relief as I finished stuffing my books in my locker. *Just two more seconds and I'll be out of here in time to escape a run-in with Ronald Rheece.* Ronald is my locker partner—and not only is he a total dork, but he also has this giant crush on me. Every time he sees me, he gets all sweet and mushy and he talks so *loudly.* I'm really worried that one of these days someone will hear him and get the wrong idea. Because, believe me, there is *no way* that I would ever go out with Ronald.

I quickly threw everything I needed into my backpack and was about to head off when a scrap of paper slipped out of my English notebook and landed on the floor.

"Hey, Jessica, you dropped something!" Ronald appeared out of nowhere and lunged for the paper. *Oh my God.* I panicked, my heart starting to pound. It was the poem I'd written about Damon!

I gulped. "Uh . . . thanks," I told him, sticking out my hand to take the poem.

4

"Hey, wait," Ronald said, glancing at the paper as he picked it up. "Is this some kind of poem?" His eyes widened with interest as he read. "It's in your handwriting—did you write this?"

"Could you please give it back?" I asked sharply. I stretched my arm over to snatch the paper away, but Ronald held it out of my reach.

"But Jessica," he said, "this is really great!" His gaze shifted from the poem to me, and on his face was that adoring expression that made me cringe.

"Ronald, that's *personal*," I said through clenched teeth. I glanced around nervously, relieved that no one seemed to be watching us. Everyone was chattering and slamming their locker doors, rushing to get to class. If only I had come to get my books a few minutes earlier, I would have missed Ronald altogether.

"I didn't know you liked to write," Ronald continued. He peered at me with his puppy-dog eyes. (Maybe that sounds appealing, but it's not. They're just big and brown and, I don't know, wet looking.)

I inhaled deeply, trying to stay calm. So Ronald had seen the love poem I wrote for Damon. Yeah, okay, that was pretty embarrassing, but as long as I could just convince him to give it back to me before—

"'Silent Love,'" Ronald read. *Out loud.* Very out loud. "Your smile melts my heart . . ."

"Shut up!" I hissed. I lunged for the paper and grabbed it out of his hand, no longer caring about making a scene. Well, as long as that scene didn't involve my poem being broadcast throughout the halls of Sweet Valley Junior High.

Ronald gave me a puzzled look. "But Jessica, you should be proud of that. 'Your smile melts my heart, your voice makes it pound,'" he repeated, his voice still horribly loud. "I like that."

I knew Ronald was a genius, but I couldn't believe he'd actually *memorized* the stupid thing already. "Listen, I have to go—"

"'Your smile melts my heart . . .'" A high, mocking voice interrupted me. "Isn't that sweet? Jessica gave the dork a love poem."

I whirled around and saw Justin Campbell standing behind me with a big smirk on his face. His best friend, Matt Springmeier, was next to him, laughing and shaking his head.

I froze. I could see my life—or at least my social life—flash before my eyes. Justin and Matt are these really obnoxious guys who think the only way to have fun is to give other people a hard time. Justin had started calling me this annoying nickname, *Lamefield*, after he'd found out I was pretending my older brother was my

6

boyfriend. That was back when Elizabeth and I had just started at SVJH after being rezoned from Sweet Valley Middle School and I had absolutely *no* friends. I thought having a high-school boyfriend would help me on the popularity front. But when Justin's crowd found out that Steven was really my brother, they made fun of me even more than they normally make fun of Ronald. That was a few months ago, and people were finally starting to forget about that whole thing. *I'd* even stopped thinking about it, now that I'd made some really cool friends like Bethel McCoy and Kristin Seltzer. But now it was coming back to haunt me.

"I—It's for English," I stammered. I glanced up at Justin's bright green eyes, the ones I actually thought were cute when I first met him. Now they just made me want to gag. "It's just an English assignment," I repeated slowly, forcing myself to breathe. I stuffed the paper into my backpack, then slung the bag over my shoulder.

"Look at that," Justin teased. He was standing pretty close to me, and I noticed that his breath smelled *really* bad. I struggled not to wrinkle my nose in disgust. "You wrote a poem about your dorky boyfriend," Justin went on. "Isn't that romantic?"

I felt my cheeks heat up. Then I stole a glance

at Ronald and cringed inwardly at the hopeful light I saw in his eyes.

"He's *not* my boyfriend," I mumbled nervously. I had to get away from them—from *all* of them, including lovesick Ronald. "Excuse me, but I have somewhere to be," I said stiffly. I spun around and started to walk briskly toward algebra class.

I groaned softly as I heard Justin's footsteps behind me. Didn't the stupid bully have anything better to do than follow me around?

"So your secret is finally out," Justin said as he reached my side. "Rheece the Geek and Lamefield are a hot item."

My worst nightmare was happening—it was just like the beginning of school all over again.

"Don't worry," Justin continued. "We won't tell anyone about you and the dork, *Lamefield*."

I shuddered as the sound of that nickname sent a terrifying chill down my back.

He laughed loudly, then turned and stalked off in the other direction, leaving me standing there in the middle of the hallway. I took a deep breath, then kept walking to my classroom, avoiding the gaze of everyone I passed.

My hands shook a little as I sank into my seat and pulled my backpack onto the desk in front of me.

I looked around as the classroom started to fill up. People were talking softly to one another as they got settled. I was relieved to find that no one was paying any attention to me.

This isn't a big deal, I tried to reassure myself. *Justin and Matt will forget about it. I mean, no one would actually believe that I wrote a love poem for Ronald Rheece, right?*

Thank goodness Damon hadn't been around. If he thought Ronald and I were a couple, then he'd never ask me out.

As if he's ever going to anyway, I thought in frustration.

At least no one knew that poem was actually for Damon. I couldn't even imagine what I would do if Damon found out. *He won't*, I thought. *Nobody will find out about the poem, and nobody will think Ronald is my boyfriend.*

All I had to do was go into major avoid-Ronald mode. The whole stupid rumor would be over in a second as long as I made sure I was never, ever seen with him.

Bethel

"Twenty-six, twenty-seven, twenty-eight." I stuck the pen in the top of the clipboard and set it down on the cafeteria table. "I still need twenty-two more signatures by tomorrow, Jess." I chewed my lip nervously. "I'll never make it."

"Yeah, sure," Jessica answered distractedly. She swirled her straw around in the full cup of soda that she'd been staring into and not drinking for the last twenty minutes. I'd never seen Jessica like this at lunch before. Usually she's ravenous and bursting to tell me the latest news.

"Okay," I said, leaning back and crossing my arms over my chest. "Is there a reason why you haven't listened to a word I've said?"

Jessica's face flushed, and she glanced at me apologetically. At least she'd heard *that* comment.

"I'm sorry, Bethel," she said hurriedly, pressing her fingertips into her temples. A strand of blond hair fell over her face, and she pushed it back behind her ear. "I think it's great that you're

running for class president. It's—I'm just tired."
She frowned, then stirred her straw around
again.

"But do you think I have a chance to actually
win?" I asked anxiously, sitting forward. "I
mean, what about this petition that all the class-
president candidates have to fill up? I still need
so many signatures."

Jessica stared across the table at me, her blue-
green eyes finally focusing on my face. "Bethel,
you work so hard," she said sincerely. "And
you're, like, the smartest person I know . . . except for my sister, obviously."

"Don't forget Ronald Rheece," I added. "He's
taking high-school classes already."

Jessica winced. "Let's not talk about him," she
said.

I raised an eyebrow. "More problems with
your wacky locker partner?" I teased.

She looked straight down at the table, tracing
the plastic pattern with her finger. "You're gonna
think it's stupid," she muttered.

I bit back a smile. Jessica cared way more
about what other people thought than I did, and
sometimes she did get upset over some pretty
silly stuff. Still, I wouldn't be friends with Jessica
if I hadn't learned that she had a lot more to her
than what's on the surface. And she had the

biggest heart, even if she didn't realize it. I'd never gotten over the time she'd taken my side and stood up to Lacey Frells, the most popular *and* obnoxious girl in the school.

"Just spit it out," I told her. "Then we can get back to my campaign."

Jessica sighed. "It was something at my locker this morning, that's all."

"What happened?" I asked, sticking a forkful of cold spaghetti in my mouth.

"Well . . ." Jessica flushed. "You know Justin Campbell and Matt Springmeier?"

I nodded. "Unfortunately," I said, setting my fork down on my plate. I stared at the heap of uneaten pasta in front of me, scrunching my nose at the thought of eating more. I didn't have much of an appetite. This whole class-president thing was really making me insane.

"Well, I kind of wrote this poem. This—well, I guess maybe you could call it a, you know, like a love poem?" she squeaked out. "For Damon," she added, not meeting my eyes.

I burst out laughing. "I'm sorry," I said when she glared at me. "But a *love poem?*"

"Okay," she said sharply. "That's not the important part anyway. I dropped the dumb poem in front of Ronald this morning, and he picked it up and read it. I mean, *out loud.*"

My eyebrows shot up. Even though I don't care what people think of me as much as Jessica does, I wouldn't want the whole school to hear something I wrote. Especially a love poem to the ninth-grader of my dreams.

"It gets worse." Jessica moaned, seeing the surprised expression on my face. "Justin Campbell and Matt Springmeier overheard, and Justin started saying that it was a love poem I'd written for *Ronald*, and that he was my boyfriend, and…" Jessica trailed off. She blinked a couple of times, like she was about to cry.

I felt a surge of anger.

"Those jerks," I said. "Where do they get off, picking on people like that?"

Jessica looked back down at the table, and I checked to see if Justin or Matt was around. Then I noticed Damon Ross, the guy Jessica is completely crazy over, sitting at a table near the juice machine. He was staring at the back of Jessica's head like it held the secret to life or something.

I grinned, then reached over to tap Jessica's arm.

"Don't turn around," I warned. "But there's something behind you that could give a serious lift to your mood."

Jessica's eyes widened, and she immediately started to twist her head around.

13

I dug into her skin with my nails. "I said *don't* turn around," I whispered. I forgot that when you tell Jessica Wakefield *not* to do something, it's kind of like giving her a green light to do it. I guess I'm kind of the same way, though. We both like a good challenge.

Jessica squirmed a little, obviously dying to look. "What is it?" she asked. "Did Lacey just make a total fool of herself?"

I smiled. "Better," I assured her. I peeked over at Damon again, and his eyes were still glued to Jessica.

"You know that guy—what's his name again?" I paused, pretending to be confused. "Oh, right, *Damon*," I said. Jessica's eyes lit up.

"Damon's here?" she asked eagerly. She immediately reached up and ran her hand through her hair to smooth it down.

"He happens to be staring right at you," I told her.

Jessica froze. "At . . . me?" she asked weakly. "Are you sure? I mean, maybe he's just staring into space or something, or maybe—"

"Jess, he's looking straight at you," I said firmly. "Now, can we get back to this petition? I was thinking maybe we could—"

"How do I look?" Jessica interrupted anxiously. "Do I have anything on my face?"

14

"Jessica, he's looking at the *back* of your head," I said slowly. "He can't see your face."

The bell rang, and I stood up, grabbing my lunch tray and my clipboard.

Jessica stood up too and quickly glanced in Damon's direction. She frowned.

"He's not watching me," she said accusingly.

"Well, he *was*," I said. "For, like, five minutes."

"What do you think it *means?*" she half moaned. "Why won't he just ask me out?"

We walked out into the hallway and started heading toward French class together.

"Look, can you get your mind off the guy for one minute?" I asked, starting to feel kind of irritated. Running for class president was a big deal to me. I figured I could count on Mary Stillwater and Ginger Walters for support and probably some of the other girls from the track team. But I really wanted Jessica's help too. She's good at coming up with catchy slogans, and she's starting to get pretty popular too. If she was on my side, my campaign would get more attention.

Jessica glanced at me in obvious surprise. "What's with you?" she asked.

I sighed and pulled Jessica over to the side of the hallway, out of the flow of people. "I just want to make sure you're going to help with my campaign," I said quietly.

15

"Oh yeah, of course," Jessica answered with a shrug. "It'll be fun," she added cheerily.

I smiled, my tensed muscles relaxing a little. "Thanks," I said, relieved. "I really want to win this."

Jessica tilted her head questioningly. "Why's it such a big deal to you anyway?" she asked.

I shrugged and shifted awkwardly. I've always had this competitive thing with my big sister, Renee. The last time she came home from college, Jessica couldn't understand why I got upset. But Renee is like the queen of perfect in everything she does. I've been compared to her all my life—in school, at track, at home. I guess I want to prove to myself that I can do something different, something that Renee never tried. That's part of the reason why I decided to run for student government. But I didn't want Jessica to think I was still obsessed with the whole beating-my-sister thing.

"Hello?" Jessica prodded when I didn't answer. "Is there something you're not telling me?"

I sighed. "I wanted to try something new," I finally replied, which was half true. "And you know I never pass up a chance for a good race," I finished with a laugh.

"Well, don't worry, you can definitely count on me," Jessica assured me with a wide smile.

I smiled back, and we started walking again, weaving our way through the crowded hall.

Even though I was kind of tense about getting enough signatures for my ballot, knowing that Jessica would be there for me gave me a lot more confidence about the election. I knew by now that if Jessica said I could count on her, I definitely could. And if I was ever actually going to be elected class president, I would need all the help I could get.

Jessica

"So, did anything interesting happen in school today?" my mom asked as we sat down to dinner that night. She helped herself to a piece of garlic bread and passed the basket to me.

I took a piece of bread and handed the basket to my brother, Steven.

"The school elections started," Elizabeth answered.

"Really? Is either of you going to run for anything?" my mother asked, glancing at Elizabeth and then me.

"There's no way either of you could win," Steven said, talking with a mouth full of bread. He paused to swallow—thankfully. "Those elections are just popularity contests."

"Thanks a lot," I said, glaring at him.

"No, I mean because you're new," he explained. "And you don't know everyone."

"One of my friends is running for class president," I said, gulping down some of my juice.

"That's right," Elizabeth agreed. "I forgot to tell you—I signed her petition today."

"Great." I placed my glass back down on the table. "I told her she shouldn't worry about getting enough signatures."

"You're kidding." Elizabeth laughed. "Kristin could get fifty signatures in about five seconds. She knows everyone."

"*Kristin?*" I practically dropped my fork. "You signed *Kristin's* petition?"

"Yeah, that's right," she replied, frowning in confusion. "I just said that."

"No, you said my *friend*," I said carefully.

"Right, your *friend* Kristin Seltzer," Elizabeth answered.

"I thought you were talking about *Bethel*," I explained. "She's running for class president too," I finished, feeling the panic rise inside me.

How come Kristin didn't tell me she was running? I wondered. I hadn't really seen her all day, except for a couple of quick hellos in the hall. But we'd talked for a while yesterday, and she never mentioned anything about running.

"I already told Bethel I'd work on her campaign," I exclaimed as I remembered my promise. "What's Kristin going to do when she finds out?"

"Kristin will understand if you already made a

19

commitment to Bethel, won't she?" my mom asked.

I let out a deep breath. "I don't know," I said dismally.

"Mom's right," Elizabeth jumped in. "Kristin is really nice, Jess. She's not the type to get angry about stuff like that."

"Maybe it would be better to tell them both you're going to stay out of it," my dad—the lawyer—suggested. "Just be completely neutral. They'll understand you're in a tough situation."

"Maybe." I felt my spirits brighten at his words, but then my shoulders sagged as I thought of something else. "But who do I vote for?" I asked in agony.

"That's why they have secret ballots," Dad pointed out. "So you can vote your conscience and no one knows who you voted for."

"That's right—they are secret, right, Liz?" I asked her excitedly. "I heard somebody say they use those voting-booth things, just like for the town elections."

"That's true," she assured me.

"Good." I sank back in my chair, finally starting to relax.

My dad started talking about elections, and before long he got off on something about one of his lawyer friends, who happens to be Ronald

Rheece's father. Just my luck that my parents hang out with the nerd of the school's family. Why couldn't they be all buddy-buddy with *Damon's* mom?

"Oh, that reminds me," my mom cut in. "Mrs. Rheece called this afternoon. She and Mr. Rheece are going to a late concert Friday night, so Ronald is going to stay over here."

My head snapped up. "What?" I cried. "You're joking, right?" I glanced at my dad in desperation. "She's joking?" I repeated hopefully.

He shrugged, then turned to my mom. "He seems like a nice kid," he told her.

I looked at Elizabeth frantically—she *had* to know what this would do to me. But Elizabeth was just calmly eating her spaghetti, as if my entire life hadn't just ended. And twins are supposed to be able to read each other's minds—*wrong.*

"Mom," I began, "isn't there anywhere else he can stay? Like, with a friend?" I stopped as I realized that Ronald probably didn't have anyone who fit that description. "What about a relative?" I continued urgently. Even superdorks like Ronald have families.

My mom shook her head. "He was going to stay with his grandmother, but she got sick," she explained. "Besides, we *are* the Rheeces' friends."

It was hard to believe she wasn't trying to torture me on purpose.

"It's just one night," Elizabeth said, staring at me in confusion. "What's the big deal?"

"Exactly," my mother said, flashing my sister a satisfied smile. "It's not a big deal." She looked at me and raised her eyebrows questioningly. "Right, Jess?"

Not a big deal. Well, sure, as long as my *life* wasn't considered "a big deal." I winced as I remembered the nasty scene at my locker this morning. My plan had been to *avoid* Ronald altogether—not have him over for a slumber party!

"Mom, Ronald Rheece is the king of dorkdom," I blurted out.

Immediately a crease appeared on my mother's forehead, and my dad cleared his throat.

"I mean, he's a nice guy," I rushed to add. "In that, you know, really nerdy kind of—" I stopped as I saw the crease deepen. "This isn't about Ronald," I said, deciding to switch gears before I got myself grounded. "It's just . . . I have, um, other plans." I shot a frantic glance at my twin. *Come on, Liz, you can jump in here and help me anytime.*

But Elizabeth just sat there, looking puzzled.

"What plans?" she asked, folding her arms across her chest.

Is it possible to divorce your twin? I wondered.

"Ronald is a perfectly nice boy, and it's a real shame that you care more about what other kids think of him than finding out the truth for yourself," my mom said, shaking her head slowly. She sounded more disappointed than angry.

It's not what people think of him—*it's what they'll think of* me! I thought in misery. Still, I hated hearing my mom talk to me in that I-thought-you-were-better-than-that voice.

"Just because Ronald is a nice enough guy doesn't mean I have to be friends with him," I argued. "Elizabeth doesn't exactly hang out with him either," I pointed out, staring at Elizabeth triumphantly.

My mother let out a loud, deep sigh. "Anyway," she said, "it's just one night. I don't see how it will hurt."

You know how nurses always tell you that right before they plunge a big needle in your arm? *Don't worry, this won't hurt a bit.*

It always hurts.

Kristin

"Hey! Wait up!" I called out as soon as I spotted Jessica, her long blond hair swinging back and forth as she walked through the school's front doors. She turned when she heard my voice and flashed me a wide grin.

I dashed up the steps to catch up with her. "Jessica," I said breathlessly. "I have to tell you something."

Jessica frowned, and I laughed.

"It's nothing *bad*," I said lightly. "Come on, I'll walk you to your locker."

"Uh, that's okay. I don't need to stop there," Jessica said with a little cough.

I shrugged. "Okay, then you can walk me to mine," I said.

We joined the mass of kids heading into the building, and Jessica followed me down the hallway.

"So anyway," I continued once we were standing in front of my locker, "I wanted to tell you that I'm running for class president."

24

Jessica seemed to stiffen. She hitched her backpack up on her shoulder and looked away, avoiding my gaze.

"Jess? Is something wrong?" I asked anxiously. I twisted my head around to see if Lacey was standing behind me, but she wasn't. Jessica was reacting exactly the way she did whenever she saw my best friend. The two of them don't exactly get along.

I faced Jessica again, narrowing my eyes in confusion. "What's up?" I asked her.

"Nothing," she said quickly. "My sister already told me you were running. That's great, Kristin. Really, uh . . . great."

Uh-oh—was she hurt that I hadn't told her sooner?

"I was going to tell you yesterday," I said hurriedly. "It's just everything was kind of crazy. I wasn't even planning on running, but then Brian brought it up and Mandy and a bunch of other people kept telling me to do it, so I just started a petition. But now I have all these signatures, and I'm actually pretty excited about it."

"Oh, it's okay," Jessica finally answered. But she was still frowning. "But—I mean, are you sure— is this really what you want?" She reached up and tucked a strand of hair behind her ear. "Class president—that's gotta be a lot of work, right?"

"Yeah," I said with a shrug. "But also a lot of fun. Wouldn't it be great to plan the dances and pep rallies and stuff? I know you're busy with track and all," I said as I opened my locker door and pulled out the books I needed. "But I really want you to help with my campaign. Brian's going to be my campaign manager," I added. "And I'm sure he'll get some other guys to help out. *Cute* guys," I added, wiggling my eyebrows up and down.

But the only response I got was a faint smile.

I know Jessica still feels like a new kid at SVJH sometimes. I figured working on my campaign would be a good way for her to get to know a lot more people. But maybe she felt shy about meeting so many of my other friends at once. I decided I had to make it seem like I *needed* her help, and then she wouldn't feel weird about it.

"Please, Jess, I could really use your help." I dropped my books into my backpack and then raised my eyes back up to hers. "Lacey won't be around, if that's what you're worried about," I said, zipping up my backpack. "She thinks student government is . . . Well, you know how Lacey is."

"It's not—this isn't about Lacey," Jessica said slowly. She sighed, then started to fidget with the sleeves of her dark blue shirt. "I guess you didn't know," she continued, pausing to take a deep breath, "but Bethel's running too."

"Ohhhh," I said slowly, finally getting why she'd been so weird this whole time. I looked away, unsure of what to say.

"Kristin, I'm *really* sorry," Jessica said quickly. "But I kind of told her I'd work on her campaign—since I didn't know you were running."

"Well, I *will* have your vote at least, right?" I joked. I didn't want Jessica to think I'd actually get mad over this. But it *was* sort of awkward, knowing that Jessica's other good friend was running against me.

"Kristin!"

I spun around at the sound of the familiar voice and saw Lacey striding toward me with an intent expression on her face. She stopped when she saw Jessica, frowned, then flipped her wavy brown hair over her shoulder and hurried over to my side without even acknowledging Jessica's presence.

"I need your help," Lacey blurted out, positioning herself between Jessica and me—with her back to Jessica, of course. "I absolutely *couldn't* do all the math homework last night. Can you come give me your answers? Quick, before the bell rings? I just need a few problems, I promise."

Kristin

I tried to catch Jessica's eye over Lacey's shoulder and make sure she knew everything was okay between us, but she was staring straight down at the floor.

"Come *on*," Lacey said, grabbing my elbow and yanking my arm. Lacey's like that—if you don't respond to her right away, she gets annoyed pretty fast. But we've been best friends since second grade, and we always try to help each other out.

"I'll see you later, Jess," I called out over my shoulder as Lacey started to drag me away.

I just hoped Jessica knew that I wasn't mad at her.

Jessica

Kristin hates me, I thought miserably as I trudged around the corner toward my locker. I needed my math book, and I was hoping Ronald would already be gone by now. He didn't like to cut it too close and risk missing the bus to his advanced-calculus class at the high school.

I paused midstride as I neared my locker, peering around the hallway to make sure there was no sign of him. Once I was satisfied that he wasn't there, I hurried over and turned the lock as quickly as possible so that I could grab my math book and get out of danger.

At least the votes are secret, I reminded myself. I could promise Kristin *and* Bethel I'd vote for them, and they'd never have to know who I actually ended up voting for.

But who will *I vote for?* I wondered.

I had no idea—for now I just had to make sure I got out of this without losing either one of my best friends.

Jessica

And I still wasn't sure about working for Bethel. It wouldn't be fair to Kristin, would it?

Dad was probably right—I should stay out of it completely.

I grabbed my math book and tossed it into my backpack, then slammed the locker door shut and turned to head to class.

I stopped in my tracks, my heart racing.

Damon Ross stood at his locker, just a few feet away. Trying to look casual, I dropped my backpack on the floor and started to rifle through it, my eyes glued to Damon. He was searching carefully through his locker, and he had the most adorable look of concentration on his face. Just being *near* him made me feel so giddy—everything else flew out of my head.

I watched as he bent down and reached into his backpack, pulling out a tiny green sweater that probably belonged to his little sister. His face broke into a half-amused, half-embarrassed smile before he stuffed the sweater in his locker.

I took a deep breath. I was going to do it—I was going to have a normal conversation with Damon Ross. Before I could lose my nerve, I strode over to him and flashed my friendliest smile.

"I think you left that sweater in the dryer too long," I said, amazed that my voice sounded so natural.

"Huh?" Damon whirled around, clearly surprised. "Oh, hi, Jessica," he said, beaming up at me. My heart jumped at the sound of his voice, and all the blood seemed to rush to my head. "It's, uh, my little sister's," he said, chuckling. "I'm not sure how it ended up in there."

"I figured," I said, grinning back at him. It was nearly impossible to look into those amazing blue eyes and still speak in normal sentences. "Nobody could shrink a sweater that much. Not even me," I managed to say. *I think I deserve bonus points for making sense and being funny,* I decided.

Damon shut his locker door and slung his backpack over his shoulder. He stared at me for a second. "So, Jessica, do you—" He paused to clear his throat.

My heart soared. This was it—Damon Ross was *finally* going to ask me out.

"Yes?" I prodded, biting my lip in anticipation. I glanced around nervously. Everyone was hurrying to finish at their lockers and get to class. The bell would ring at any second—I just hoped it would wait a *little* longer.

"Jessica! Hey, Jessica, I need to talk to you!" a voice yelled from behind us.

No, this can't be, I thought in horror. Why wasn't Ronald on the bus already?

I gulped, then turned slowly and saw Ronald rushing down the hallway toward me, his big red jacket flapping out around him.

I spun back to look at Damon, who was watching Ronald with a curious expression. I *couldn't* let Damon hear Ronald talk to me in his usual mushy way. Damon would get completely the wrong idea. I couldn't even stand to think that Damon might actually believe I was already going out with Ronald—of all people!

"Uh, I'd better go," I told Damon hurriedly, not meeting his eyes. "I'll talk to you later, okay?"

Damon shrugged, then nodded. "See ya," he said quietly before strolling away down the hallway.

Every part of me wanted to chase after him and beg him to finish what he had started to ask me. But I couldn't risk letting him hear Ronald say something that would put me in the loser-impossible-to-ever-ask-me-out hall of fame.

"What is it?" I snapped as Ronald reached my side.

"I thought I saw you from down the hall," Ronald said breathlessly. "I guess you got to our locker late, so I missed you before." Ronald said "our locker" as if it were something precious we owned together. I shuddered.

"Yeah, too bad," I muttered.

"I know." Ronald grinned as if he thought I was truly sorry for the missed opportunity of a bonding locker moment. I cringed inwardly as I thought about the *real* missed opportunity of the morning. . . .

Ronald dug into his pocket and then pulled out a photograph and thrust it at me. "I wanted to show you this," he said eagerly.

I glanced at the picture but didn't take it from him. It looked like some kind of model of a building or something. "Nice," I responded as enthusiastically as I would praise one of my brother's nerdy model airplanes. I started to walk down the hallway, but Ronald scurried after me.

"Thanks," he said, oblivious to my lack of excitement. "It's one of my matchstick castles," he explained. "I make them out of, you know, matchsticks. . . ."

"No kidding," I answered, my eyes flitting around the hall to make sure Justin and his sidekick, Matt, weren't in the area. No sign of them, and in fact there weren't many people around at all—it was almost time for class. I quickened my pace, and Ronald rushed along beside me.

"Anyway," Ronald continued, "I wanted to show you the picture because I thought maybe you'd like to see one of these up close."

Jessica

The bell began to blare out of the speakers on the walls, and for once I was totally grateful for that annoying warning to get to class.

"You know," Ronald continued, raising his voice to be heard over the bell, "I could bring it over on Fri—"

"Sure, that sounds great," I interrupted briskly. *Don't say it*, I thought. *Don't say you're coming to my house on Friday.* I couldn't bear for even the few stragglers walking near us to hear Ronald announce our weekend plans. "You're going to miss your bus, though," I added.

Ronald nodded. "Thanks," he said, beaming at me as if I'd done him some kind of huge favor. "I'll see you at our locker." Then he dashed off in the direction of the parking lot.

I closed my eyes briefly, willing myself to stay calm, and continued in the direction of my math class. The second bell went off, and I broke into a slow jog. It's not like I've never been late to class before, but right now the last thing I wanted was to attract attention to myself.

As long as I keep a low profile, I might not wind up the laughingstock of the whole school.

Bethel

I strode into the principal's office after first period, gripping my petition tightly in my hand. I'd just barely gotten enough signatures. I never really hang out with my classmates much. I kind of do my own thing—I'm not part of any of the big groups. I'm happy that way. I mean, I have friends I like, and I don't have to spend time around anyone I don't *want* to be with. But it's kind of strange to have to *work* to find fifty people to sign a petition for you.

Still, all that mattered was that I'd *made* it. I was trying to look at this election like a cross-country race—as long as I could hang in there for the rough parts, I'd break out with a burst of speed in the end, when it counted, and get the win.

"Hi, Mrs. Adams," I said to the junior-high secretary as I handed her my crinkled petition.

"You're running for class president?" she asked after glancing down at the page.

"Yeah," I said.

"That's wonderful," Mrs. Adams responded, smiling back at me. I relaxed, unclenching my hands, which had tightened into fists at my sides.

"Well, if I don't get any other petitions in the next few minutes, you may win the presidency by default. I've got four people running for ninth-grade president and two for seventh grade, but so far no one else seems interested in being eighth-grade president."

"Really?" I frowned in disappointment. I didn't want to win that way—what good was a race without any competition?

The door to the office squeaked open, and I turned around to see Kristin Seltzer. I tensed up again as my eyes traveled down to the pile of papers in Kristin's hand. What was *she* doing here?

Kristin glanced at me with a smile. "Hey, Bethel," she greeted me.

Kristin's the total opposite of me. She acts like she's friends with everyone, and most people think that's cool, but it kind of makes me uncomfortable.

"Hello, Kristin, what brings you here?" Mrs. Adams asked.

"I'm running for class president," Kristin

answered. She approached Mrs. Adams's desk and dropped her pile of papers onto it.

My heart sank. I wanted someone to compete against—but did it have to be one of the most popular girls in our class?

"Kristin, you only needed fifty signatures, you know," Mrs. Adams said as she flipped through the pages of Kristin's petition. She chuckled. "This is more than enough to get you on the ballot."

Kristin's cheeks flushed, and she smiled shyly. I almost snorted at her pathetic attempt to look humble. I don't know how Jessica can be friends with such a fake. How typical of her to run around getting a million more signatures than she needed, just to show off how many people she knows.

"I gave it to some people, and then they kept passing it around," Kristin replied with a small shrug. She raised her gaze up to meet mine, and I narrowed my eyes to show I didn't buy her act.

"Well, good luck to you both," Mrs. Adams said, returning her attention to the paperwork on her desk.

"Thanks," Kristin answered. "I'll see ya, Bethel." She turned and bounced out of the office in her usual perky way.

I sighed as I followed her out, shaking my

head. Unfortunately I really *was* going to need a lot of luck, now that I knew who my opponent was.

At least I have Jessica, I told myself as I rounded the corner toward the locker room. Even though Jessica's new, she already seems to know more people than I do, and she has that cheerleader spirit, like Kristin—except that *Jessica* has some brains to go with it.

As long as Jessica's on my side, I still have a chance.

Damon

**Reasons why Jessica always
leaves to talk to Ronald Rheece
when I try to ask her out:**

1. I had something disgusting in my teeth.
2. My breath smelled really bad.
3. My fly was unzipped.
4. She . . . likes Ronald?

It's pretty scary when you're actually hoping
you grossed out the girl you like.

Bethel

"What do you mean, you can't help me?" I said, letting go of my shoelaces and staring up at Jessica.

"I'm sorry," Jessica muttered. She sat down next to me on the locker-room bench, twisting her hands together nervously. "I know I told you I would, but that was before I knew Kristin was running. I can't get in the middle like that—I told her I wouldn't help her either."

I bent down and yanked at my shoelaces again, tying them into a tight bow. I could feel the hurt rising up inside me. When I'd found out that Kristin was running for class president too, it never even crossed my mind that Jessica's friendship with her would be a problem. Because Jessica had already *promised* me she'd help. She knew I needed her way more than Kristin did!

"But Jess," I argued. "Kristin doesn't *need* any help. You should have seen the petition she handed in today. She had almost everyone's signature in the entire world." I shook my

40

head. "Kristin thinks that just because she tries to be friends with the whole school, she'd be a good president, but it takes more than just being *popular*. You actually have to be able to think about things besides what to do on Saturday night."

Jessica frowned, then leaned down to lace up her trainers. "Kristin's not like that," she said. "She has ideas, like fun things that would get everyone involved."

"*Fun things?*" I echoed. "Jess, student government isn't one big party."

Jessica finished tying her shoelaces and stood up with a loud sigh. "I don't know what you have against Kristin," she said. "I wish you could see how nice she is."

I pressed my lips together, restraining myself from saying anything else. It was obvious that for whatever reason, Jessica couldn't see Kristin for what she really was—fake.

I glanced up at the clock on the wall and realized we were late for practice. "Come on," I said. "Let's get out there before Coach Krebs comes looking for us."

We were both silent as we left the locker room and made our way through the gym to the exit outside.

"Are you still mad at me?" Jessica asked in a

small voice as we stepped out into the bright fall sunshine. The day was crisp and clear with just a bit of a breeze—perfect running weather.

"No." I shook my head. We broke into a slow jog, heading toward the track. "I'm not mad. You're probably doing the right thing." *At least, you would be if your friend Kristin, aka Miss Popularity, wasn't about to totally crush me in the elections,* I added inwardly. "But I am worried about how I'm going to beat Kristin," I said glumly.

"Well, you've got Mary and Ginger, right? And isn't Jan helping you too?" Jessica asked, picking up the pace a little as we neared the field, where our teammates were already warming up. "And you got all the signatures you needed. That's something, right?" she said encouragingly.

"I hope so," I said. "What I really need, though, is a campaign theme—whatever it's called—a platform. Something that will really get everyone's attention."

"You'll figure something out," Jessica assured me.

We joined the rest of the team, and Jessica and I started to stretch.

What would *my platform be?* I wondered for the millionth time in the past week. What could I possibly say that would help me beat the most popular girl in our class, when I knew the elections were total popularity contests?

Maybe that's it, I realized with a start. Maybe I wasn't the only one who thought it was ridiculous to choose a class president based on popularity alone. Maybe I had a campaign theme after all. I would run on the *un*popular ticket, and this would be my message: There's a choice—you don't have to vote for someone just because you know who they are. Instead you can vote for someone who really cares about leading the class—me.

Jessica

Dear Diary,

   So, I took this daffodil off the kitchen table and decided to play that silly game, the one where you pick the petals off to figure out if a guy likes you or not. Only my question was if Damon was actually going to ask me out yesterday. Here's what happened: He was, he wasn't, he was, he wasn't, he was . . . he wasn't. Can you believe that? It ended on no! So then I realized that I should really go for two out of three, but Mom came in and said not to wreck her flower arrangement. How can a stupid flower know anything anyway?

Bethel's Eighth-Grade Class-President Speech

There are many reasons why I am qualified to be our class president. For instance . . .

It's important that a class president know and respect all of the people in the class, and that's why I . . .

As a member of our school's track team, I have learned skills that would help me as a class president, such as . . .

Vote for me if you want a president who knows how to do more than just be popular and look pretty.

Jessica

"Hello?" I answered the phone quickly, praying that it was Ronald calling to cancel tonight's little sleep over. It was Friday night— the time I'd been dreading since my mom's announcement at dinner on Wednesday. I'd had this secret hope the past couple of days that somehow a weird shifting-of-the-universe thing would happen this week and we'd just skip over Friday. But unfortunately the universe doesn't seem to shift easily—especially not for me.

"Jessica? Hi!"

"Kristin?" I sat up straighter. I'd barely talked to Kristin since she'd told me she was running for president. "What's up?" I asked, settling back in my bed.

"This election stuff is crazy," Kristin answered. "I can't talk long 'cause Brian and some other people are here to work on posters. There's *so* much to do."

I winced. Was this her way of letting me know that she was still upset I wasn't helping?

I heard someone laugh in the background, and Kristin asked me to hang on while she went to talk to whoever it was.

I felt a knot in the pit of my stomach. It sounded like they were having a lot of fun—I wished I could be there. But then I felt guilty for even wishing it since I wasn't helping Bethel. I sighed. My life would be a lot easier when this whole stupid campaign was over.

"Anyway," Kristin said, coming back to the phone, "I was wondering if maybe you could meet a bunch of us at the movies later. No campaign stuff—I promise."

My heart jumped. Why would she invite me out if she was mad at me? I could still hang out with Kristin and everyone else over there, without getting involved in the election.

Just as I was about to say yes, I remembered Ronald, and the knot in my stomach tightened. There was no way my parents would let me go out while he was here. Besides, I couldn't let Lizzie suffer alone. Thanks to Ronald Rheece, I'd have to miss out on the movies too.

"Thanks, but—I promised my mom I'd, uh, help her clean the kitchen cabinets." It felt weird lying to Kristin, but I couldn't tell her the truth. What if she hung up and told all her cool friends that Jessica Wakefield couldn't come to the movies because she had plans with Ronald Rheece?

"Bummer," Kristin said. "Can't you get out of it? I mean, it's Friday night. Tell her you'll do it tomorrow or something."

"I can't," I said. "She's . . . she really wants it done tonight," I finished, hoping Kristin would just let it go.

"Oh, okay, then," she said, sounding pretty disappointed. I frowned. This was the second time I'd let her down recently—how long would it take before she gave up on me?

Elizabeth opened my door and stuck her head in. "Jess, the Rheeces are here," she said loudly.

I put my finger to my lips and shook my head, desperately trying to get her to be quiet.

Elizabeth raised her eyebrows, then shook her head and left, shutting the door behind her.

"Did she say the Rheeces?" Kristin asked.

I winced. "No, no, not the Rheeces," I said hastily, my palms starting to sweat. "The, uh, Reeslings. They're old friends of the family. Yeah, uh, Martin and Susan Reesling. I guess they just stopped by. They do that sometimes," I babbled.

"Hey, that's great," Kristin said. "Then you won't have to do the cabinets, right? Maybe you can just make an appearance and then escape."

"Actually, I really have to stick around now," I said. "My parents don't like us going out when we have company," I added. "So I guess you probably have to get back to work."

"Yeah," Kristin said quietly. She sounded kind of hurt.

But what if Ronald came running up to my room, yelling my name? I had to hang up! "I'll talk to you later, then," I said, wishing I could explain.

We hung up, and I breathed a sigh of relief. *That was a close call.*

For a minute I sat there, chewing on my nails. Finally I got up and found my bottle of Electric Raspberry nail polish. I rolled the bottle between my hands, then sat down at my desk and started to paint each nail slowly and carefully.

I knew I had to leave my room eventually. I just didn't see any point in rushing it. What was I supposed to do with Ronald at my house all night long? It made me sick just thinking about going downstairs.

Wakefield House, Friday Night

6:45 P.M. Elizabeth yells through Jessica's door that Ronald is asking for her downstairs. Jessica says she'll be out as soon as she's finished painting her nails.

6:55 P.M. Elizabeth returns to Jessica's room. Jessica promises that she only needs three more coats, and then she'll come down as soon as her nails are dry.

6:56 P.M. Elizabeth rattles the door handle and insists that Jessica let her in. Jessica claims she can't open the door because she'll mess up her nails.

6:57 P.M. Elizabeth points out that she can just come in through the bathroom door that connects their bedrooms.

6:58 P.M. Jessica warns Elizabeth that nail-polish fumes are very toxic. In fact, her throat is starting to really itch. Maybe she should just stay in bed.

6:59 P.M. Elizabeth responds that if that's true, Jessica should leave the room and come downstairs right away. Jessica promises she's coming, and Elizabeth leaves.

7:10 P.M.   Elizabeth bursts into Jessica's room through the bathroom and threatens to bring Ronald *in* if Jessica won't come *out*.

7:11 P.M.   Jessica looks around her room at the pile of clean underwear waiting to be put away, the magazines scattered everywhere, open to articles like "Does He Like You? Ten Telltale Signs" and "No-Fail Flirt Secrets." She imagines Ronald blabbing away to her in school on Monday about the fact that he was in her bedroom and grudgingly follows her sister downstairs.

Kristin

"Where do you want to sit?" Brian asked me, his green eyes wide and questioning.

"What?" I put a couple of pieces of popcorn in my mouth and surveyed the nearly empty movie theater, then looked back at Brian. Usually when we saw movies together, he'd just plop down close to the front and I'd follow him there, even though I kind of liked the back better. He'd *never* asked me where I wanted to sit before.

Somehow this whole going-to-the-movies-with-Brian thing felt superstrange tonight. At first I thought a bunch of people were supposed to come too, but then everyone else bailed. Even Jessica. So it ended up just me and Brian. That shouldn't have been a problem since Brian and I have been going to the movies together for as long as we've been friends, which is practically forever.

But lately I wasn't so sure—that we were just friends, I mean. I've had a huge crush on Brian for a while, and recently he's been acting like maybe he feels the same way. Unless I'm just imagining the whole thing.

"So, where do you want to go?" Brian repeated. He reached into our giant bucket of popcorn and grabbed a few pieces, then tossed them in his mouth.

"Uh, here's fine," I said, pointing to the row of seats next to where we stood.

Brian shrugged, then walked into the row, sitting down in a seat near the middle. I sat down next to him and set the popcorn on my lap.

"I hope the previews are good," I said as I shifted around, trying to get comfortable. Brian started to spread out, but then his knee brushed against mine and he quickly moved his leg back. I placed my elbow down on the armrest between our seats and immediately bumped into his arm. We both pulled back, then tried again and knocked into each other for a second time. I hesitated and then giggled, nudging him really hard with my elbow.

"Hey, when did you become such a big armrest hog?" he joked.

I blushed. "I guess the same time you did," I answered, feeling embarrassed for no reason. "Want some more popcorn?" I held out the bucket, and he took a big handful, stuffing it in his mouth. As he chewed, a strand of his longish blond hair fell in front of his face, and I almost reached out to push it back, like I did all the time. But something made me keep my hand still, and he finally shoved it behind his ear himself.

The lights dimmed as the screen lit up with the first preview, and I settled deeper into my seat. I cast a quick sidelong glance at our shared armrest and saw that it was free, so I leaned my elbow on it. But Brian put his elbow there at the same time, and we touched *again*.

I held my breath, waiting for him to move. *Or should I move?* It was kind of nice, though, feeling his arm against mine. It made my skin warm, and it made me sort of warm inside too.

The previews kept running, and I relaxed my arm a little, letting it rest against his.

The movie started, and I still didn't move away—and neither did he.

Jessica

I took a deep breath before stepping into the family room, telling myself that the best thing was just to get this night over with. Ronald sat on the couch, watching some nature program on TV, a can of soda on the coffee table in front of him. He reached for the soda and looked up at me at the same time, managing to knock the can over *and* smash his knee into the coffee table. Soda spilled everywhere as Ronald let out a little yelp of pain.

I winced, suddenly suspecting that this was going to be the longest night of my life.

"Hi, Jessica," Ronald said, clutching his knee and dabbing at the table with a napkin.

"Hi," I said, frozen in place.

"Don't worry about that, Ronald," Elizabeth said, gesturing at the soda spill. "I'll take care of it." She ran into the kitchen.

Still holding his knee, Ronald flashed me a big grin. "Your house is really nice," he said.

I shrugged and dropped down onto the far end of the couch. "Thanks," I answered, licking my lips nervously. *Be careful,* I warned myself. *Don't be too friendly, or Ronald might think you're flirting or something.*

"So what do you want to do tonight?" Ronald asked eagerly. I glanced over at his hopeful expression and bit back a grimace.

"I guess we'll just watch TV," I said casually. I grabbed the remote and started to flip through the channels aimlessly.

"I brought that castle to show you," Ronald went on. "You know, the one I made with matchsticks." He gestured toward a shoe box on the coffee table.

"Great," I said, still channel surfing. If I could just find a good show that would hold Ronald's attention, maybe he would stop talking to me.

"You want to see it?" he asked, reaching for the shoe box.

"Yeah, sure. Whatever." I craned my neck around, trying to see into the kitchen. Where was Elizabeth anyway?

Out of the corner of my eye I saw Ronald take the cover off the shoe box. He lifted something out and set it on the coffee table.

Elizabeth finally walked in the room, carrying a sponge and a roll of paper towels. "Wow!" she exclaimed when she saw Ronald's castle. "Where'd you get that?"

At least if my sister paid Ronald enough attention, maybe he'd leave me alone.

"I made it," Ronald announced proudly. "I brought it over to show Jessica. Don't you want to see, Jessica?"

I sighed and dropped the remote down on the sofa, then scooted over to check out the castle.

My eyes widened in surprise when I focused in on the model. It was actually a perfect miniature castle, about six inches tall, with turrets and even a drawbridge. And it really was made out of wooden matchsticks, except for a few little metal things glued onto it in places. I hadn't expected the castle to look so, well, *good.*

"Wow!" I said, echoing Elizabeth.

The tips of Ronald's ears turned pink. He grinned, obviously pleased. "Do you like it? Really?" he asked.

"Are you kidding?" Elizabeth asked before I could respond. "This is really amazing, Ronald."

I nodded reluctantly. "Yeah, it is," I admitted. Not that I was a huge fan of matchstick model castles or anything, but it was pretty cool that Ronald had made it himself.

"Watch this," Ronald said, turning a little metal crank. The drawbridge, which was held by heavy thread wrapped around little metal knobs, slowly opened.

I nodded. "That's cool," I agreed. It really was.

"I can't believe it works," Elizabeth added.

Ronald looked so pleased, I thought he might

explode or something. It kind of made me feel bad, seeing how little it took to make him light up like this.

"Where'd you get those metal things for the drawbridge?" I asked.

"Different places," Ronald said. "Hardware stores and craft stores. My mom goes to flea markets sometimes and brings me back old junk jewelry so I can use the pieces. Like, see the handle on the crank? That's actually an earring back."

I looked at it closely. "Oh yeah," I said. "I've seen that kind before."

"How'd you know to use it like that?" Elizabeth asked.

Ronald shrugged. "I don't know. I just look at things and try to think what they could be, you know, in miniature. I make miniatures out of other stuff too. Not just matchsticks." He laughed, sounding embarrassed. "I know it's kind of a weird hobby, but it's fun."

"I think it's great," I said, smiling encouragingly.

"So, what do you guys want to do?" Elizabeth asked.

I stared down at the remote control. Ronald wasn't the most exciting guy in the world to spend Friday night with, but my mom was right—it wouldn't kill me just to let him have fun this one night of his life. He was probably used to spending his weekends looking up math problems on the Web or something. I picked up the remote and clicked off the TV.

"Why don't we let Ronald decide?" I suggested.

The three of us walked over to the hall closet with all our family's board games, and Ronald immediately picked out—surprise!—Trivial Pursuit. Not exactly my favorite, but I didn't mind.

We sat down to play, and of course Ronald barely missed any questions. I knew he was one of the smartest kids at SVJH, but still—this game tested such totally random stuff. I didn't think it was possible for anyone to know that much.

"Okay, which category this time?" I asked Ronald at his next turn.

Ronald landed on Geography.

I pulled out a card and read it to myself silently. Then I glanced up, grinning triumphantly. "You'll never get this one," I promised. "'Where is the only place in the world where a boat can sail under a train driving under a car driving under an airplane?'"

"Easy," Ronald said with a satisfied smile. "The Longfellow Bridge in Boston." He put another wedge in his pie-shaped game piece and rubbed his hands together.

Elizabeth's jaw dropped. "How did you *know* that?" she asked.

"Well . . ." Ronald looked up at us sheepishly.

"I kind of got that question when I played with my cousin last week."

"That's cheating," I complained.

"I can't help it if I have a photographic memory for totally useless information," Ronald protested. We all laughed, and Elizabeth and I exchanged a surprised look. Ronald could actually make fun of himself—pretty cool.

"Oh yeah—like advanced calculus, right?" I teased.

"Hey! Advanced calculus isn't useless," Ronald objected, still grinning. "How else would you figure out the centroid of a parabola?" he asked innocently.

I rolled my eyes. "Oh yeah," I said jokingly, "just this morning I found this parabola, and I was *desperate* to figure out its—its centroid thingie."

Ronald started to laugh again, his eyes warm and bright. It was nice seeing him this happy, though I felt a twinge of worry as I reminded myself not to be *too* nice.

It was my turn next, and I got sports and games. Elizabeth grabbed the card and read aloud, "'According to superstition, what can you place on a Ouija board to prevent evil spirits from coming through?'"

I grinned. "A silver coin. Remember—we used to play with the Ouija board, Liz."

She giggled. "Yeah. I thought it was pretty cool until that time when we asked it where our great-grandmother is buried and it gave us the right answer even though we didn't know it."

"That's right," I said. "We never used it after that."

"Weird," Ronald said. "But you probably just knew the answer subconsciously."

"No way," I argued. "We were only, like, ten years old."

"There's got to be a scientific explanation," Ronald persisted.

I groaned, crossing my arms over my chest. "Science isn't *everything*, Ronald. Right, Liz?"

Elizabeth nodded. "I know what you mean," she told him. "But Jessica's telling the truth—the Ouija board did work."

Ronald still looked doubtful. "If you're ever going to really trust something, you have to test it scientifically. You know, at the Future Scientists of America club, we—"

"So then why don't we test it?" I interrupted.

"I don't know," Elizabeth began. "Maybe we should just—"

"It would be fun," I pleaded, giving her my sweet, adoring twin face, the one she could never refuse.

"Okay," she relented.

I hopped up to get the Ouija board from the hall closet.

But how am I going to ask it what I'm dying to know without hurting Ronald's feelings? I wondered.

61

Conversations with a Ouija Board

Elizabeth turns out the lights. Ronald, Jessica, and Elizabeth sit in a tight circle, the Ouija board resting on their legs, hands on the planchette. For several minutes nothing happens.

Ronald: I thought so! This doesn't work. It's totally unscien—

The planchette moves. Jessica lets out a little shriek. Then silence. The planchette spells out h-e-l-l-o.

Ronald immediately accuses the twins of moving the planchette. Jessica tells him to be quiet.

Elizabeth: Are you good or evil?
Ouija: G-o-o-d
Jessica: See? The silver dime works.
Elizabeth: Can you predict the future?
Ouija: S-o-m-e-t-i-m-e-s
Jessica: Does Bethel have a chance in the election?
Elizabeth: Will the *Zone* work out?
Jessica: Shhh! I asked first.

The planchette starts to move again. Ronald makes both Jessica and Elizabeth swear they aren't doing it.

Ouija:	Yes
Jessica:	Yes to Bethel or yes to the *Zone*?
Ronald:	Will I get an A in advanced calculus this marking period?
Elizabeth:	Wait, what about the *Zone*?
Ouija:	Yes
Jessica:	Everyone stop asking at once! Now, in the very near future is something that, uh, someone in this room has wished for involving, uh, a certain someone going to happen?
Ouija:	Yes

Jessica smiles to herself. Then she notices Ronald looking at her with a strange, hopeful gleam in his eye.

Ronald (nervously clearing his throat): Does someone in this room have strong feelings for . . . uh . . . someone else?

Jessica (jumps up, upsetting the board): This is stupid. Let's do something else.

Ronald: But it was just getting good!

Jessica

"Uh-oh," I said to Elizabeth when I noticed Ronald's matchstick castle on the kitchen table early Saturday morning. "I guess Ronald left this in here after he showed it to Mom last night. I'd better bring it out to him before his parents get here."

I picked up the castle and carried it into the living room carefully. "I figured you wouldn't want to forget this," I called out as I stepped into the room.

Ronald jumped up and tossed a T-shirt over something on the coffee table. When I turned to set the castle down on the bookshelf next to me, he snatched the shirt back up again and something brown and fuzzy fell out onto the floor—a teddy bear.

Ronald froze, then plucked up the bear and stuffed it into the bag he was packing. His face went from its usual pale shade to deep scarlet. He cleared his throat, looking at me nervously.

"Oh, can I see that?" I said, hoping to avoid

an awkward moment. "I love teddy bears."

Ronald watched me with obvious confusion. "You don't—you're not laughing?" he asked in a puzzled tone.

"Of course not," I assured him, smiling. Just a few more minutes and my overnight with Ronald would be history. If I could just let him leave in a good mood, I'd have nothing on my conscience *and* I'd be free.

Ronald shifted nervously, then he handed me the teddy bear. It was dark brown, and there was a button where one of its eyes had been.

"Some people might think it's dumb, carrying around a teddy bear when you're fourteen," Ronald muttered.

"I think it's sweet," I said honestly. I didn't exactly picture the man of my dreams walking around with a teddy bear or anything, but for someone like Ronald . . . well, it gave him more of a human touch. I noticed the bear's plastic nose had teeth marks on it and moved my hands down so that I wasn't touching the face anymore. "I hope you've outgrown chewing on his nose, though," I teased.

"Oh yeah, I gave that up a while ago." He grinned, and his skin color began to return to normal. "My mom says when I was a baby, she bought me all kinds of teething rings, but all I wanted to teethe on was Mr. . . . I mean, the bear's . . . nose."

I bent over to carefully place the teddy bear down on the table, then quickly brushed my palms against the sides of my jeans. As soon as Ronald was out the door, I'd be in the bathroom, scrubbing my hands with soap. All those grimy Ronald germs on that thing . . .

"You had him since you were a baby?" I asked, glancing out the window to check for the Rheeces' car.

"Since I was six months old," Ronald replied. "I dragged him around everywhere until I was about six. I even refused to go to nursery school until my mom said I could take him. The teacher made me leave him in my backpack, but every once in a while, during the day, I'd run over to my cubby and make sure he was still there."

I fought not to giggle at the image of little Ronnie lugging his teddy bear around with him everywhere. It was a funny thought—but I didn't want to hurt his feelings. "What's his name?" I asked.

Ronald shook his head. "It's stupid," he said quickly. "I mean, I was only two when I named him. It's just, you know, a dumb name."

"Oh, come on." I tilted my head to one side imploringly, curious to hear what kind of crazy name Ronald would come up with. "I won't tell anyone. Not even Elizabeth." Okay, so I'm not too good at keeping stuff from my sister, but I know that Elizabeth would never tease Ronald or anything. She and I could just have a good laugh between the two of us.

Ronald sighed. "If anyone at school ever found out . . ." He stopped and looked down at his feet. "People are mean enough already," he finished softly.

I felt a tug of guilt as I thought about the way everyone made fun of Ronald and how I didn't really do much to stop it. I'd never realized Ronald actually *minded,* though.

"Like Justin and Matt?" I asked. Ronald nodded. "You don't think I'd ever tell those guys anything, do you?" I said. "I'm not like that."

"I know you're not. I never thought you were," Ronald said quickly.

"So, then tell me," I said.

"It's Mr. Tummy," Ronald blurted out, his face flushing again.

A giggle escaped my mouth. "Mr. Tummy? Really?" Ronald's face went bright red again. "I mean, I think it's cute," I said hastily. "Really, I do. It's sweet."

Ronald smiled and seemed to relax a little. "And you promise you won't tell?"

"Not a soul," I swore solemnly.

Bethel McCoy's Campaign Poster

*8 Things I'll Do for 8th-Graders When I
Become President of the 8th Grade*

1. Boost attendance for sports events
2. Start spirit days for sports teams on game days
3. Ask for new uniforms for teams
4. Demand that more healthy foods are served in the cafeteria
5. Raise money for better equipment in the science lab
6. Organize class trips to places everyone wants to go
7. Make sure that each member of the class appears the same number of times in the yearbook
8. Hold votes on all decisions so that each member of the class feels that their voice has been heard

Don't let this election be a popularity contest. Vote for *BETHEL MCCOY* as your class president—the candidate with *real* ideas!

Jessica

"Hey, Jess."

I jumped, almost banging my head on my locker shelf.

I whirled around, relieved to see Kristin's smiling face.

It was Monday morning, and I was pretty anxious about being back in school and having to see Ronald. Knowing him, he'd immediately start blabbing away about the fantastic time he had at my house on Friday night. My reputation was on shaky enough ground. If Justin and Matt found out Ronald had slept over at my house, they'd have a field day. And I'm sure they'd come up with even worse names for me than *Lamefield.*

"Hi. How was the movie?" I asked, hoping she wasn't mad about the lame excuses I'd given her on Friday night.

Kristin's cheeks turned pink, and she glanced around the hallway, avoiding my eyes. "Uh . . . yeah, it was—um, I think it was good," she answered in a strange voice. "Anyway, I have to go finish hanging up these posters." She gestured down at the bag of posters and tape on the floor next to her. "Check it out," she said, pointing at the wall next to me. I followed her gaze to where one of her posters was hanging. It was really bright and colorful, and it said Kristin Seltzer for Eighth-Grade President, then Seltzer Sparkles below that, with pictures of seltzer bottles decorated with glitter around the words.

"Do you like it?" Kristin asked.

I nodded. "It's cool," I told her, watching as she looked at Bethel's poster higher up on the wall and then frowned. I'd been afraid she would take Bethel's message the wrong way— the last part kind of sounded like Bethel was saying Kristin didn't have a brain, that she was only running because she was popular. I knew Bethel didn't mean that, though. At least, I hoped she didn't.

"I just wish Bethel wasn't making this personal," Kristin said quietly. I glanced at her more closely and saw the hurt in her eyes. It would be so much easier if Bethel and Kristin could just get along!

"Oh, look—the edges are curling up on this one," she said, reaching out to press her poster back against the wall.

"I'll fix it," I volunteered, eager to prove I

could still be a good friend. I grabbed the tape out of her bag and ripped off pieces, then reinforced the parts of the poster coming away from the wall.

"Thanks, Jess," Kristin said happily.

"No problem," I assured her, turning around with a smile. Then I saw someone standing behind Kristin, and the smile fell off my face.

Bethel.

I watched, frozen, as her expression changed from shock to anger. As soon as she caught my eye, she turned and ran off in the opposite direction. My heart dropped as I realized that she must think I was helping Kristin with her campaign after all.

"Jess? Is something wrong?" I focused in on Kristin's worried gaze, trying to decide what to do. If I went after Bethel, maybe I could explain.

I let out a little groan. "I should go," I told Kristin. I slung my backpack over my shoulder and shut my locker door. "Good luck with the posters, okay?"

She frowned. I could tell she thought I was brushing her off. But I had to catch up with Bethel.

"I'll see ya," Kristin said, picking up her posters and strolling away with one final, confused glance.

Jessica

I shut my eyes for a second, trying to figure out what to say to Bethel. I knew I hadn't done anything wrong, but Bethel can be pretty stubborn sometimes.

"Jessica?"

My eyes opened, and I saw Ronald standing in front of me. Fate clearly had it in for me. I was just going to have to accept that.

"Hi, Ronald," I said grimly.

"I had an awesome time at your house on Friday!" Ronald practically shouted. Was it me, or did his voice sound extra loud today?

"Ronald, I'm right here," I said, gritting my teeth. "You don't have to yell." I glanced quickly in the direction of Damon's locker, relieved that he wasn't there.

My backpack started to slide down my arm, and Ronald immediately reached out to grab it before it fell on the floor. He pushed it back onto my shoulder, staring into my eyes with a ridiculously moony expression. My patience was running very thin.

"I wanted you to know what a great time I had at your house, Jessica," Ronald repeated, still yelling. Was he doing it on purpose? Was he on some kind of mission to let the whole world know that I'd wasted a Friday night playing board games with him?

"Shhh! You don't have to shout," I said in an irritated tone.

Ronald's eyes got all big and sad.

"I had fun too," I mumbled guiltily.

Ronald smiled up at me as if I'd just told him I loved him or something. He was so close, I could see little flecks of spit in the corner of his mouth, but that didn't stop him from talking as if I were in another state.

"It was just so cool hanging out together. I could have stayed up with you all night long!" he said.

He *was* doing it on purpose. He had to be. *He must want the school to think he's my boyfriend!* I realized. How dare he?

"Be quiet!" I hissed. "I can hear you." I glanced around. It was not my imagination—people were *definitely* staring at us.

But Ronald just barreled on. "I still can't believe that Oui—oof!"

I stuck my elbow in his bony little ribs. "Shut up!" I forced the words out between clenched teeth just as I stole another peek at Damon's locker.

He's there. I gulped as an intense pressure built up in my head. Damon was looking right at us, and I knew what he was wondering: *What's up between Jessica and Ronald?* I could see it in his puzzled, surprised expression.

Ronald stared at me. "What? What's the matter?"

"Just lower your voice," I pleaded.

Understanding dawned on Ronald's face. "Oh, I get it," he said. "You don't want people to know about the . . . you know, what we were doing." He nudged me on the arm as if we were both in on some huge secret. More people started to watch us, obviously hoping to catch on to our big secret.

My heart began to thump wildly, and my head was spinning.

"Stop!" I cried. "Just stop, okay? Do you want me to tell everyone that you sleep with a teddy bear named Mr. Tummy?"

Just as the words came out of my mouth, the noise level in the hall dropped like a scene in a movie or something. My hand flew to my mouth, and I wished I could erase that moment. Ronald's face turned absolutely, eerily white. He was watching me with a horrified expression that made me want to sink right into the floor.

"Aww, now, isn't that cute?"

Every muscle in my body tensed at the sound of that taunting, jeering voice. It couldn't be—it wasn't possible. I took a deep breath, then slowly turned my head and saw Justin Campbell striding up to Ronald from his locker down the hall. "Ronnie has a little teddy bear. I'll bet

74

Ronnie still sucks his thumb too," Justin said mockingly.

I backed up a few steps, my pulse racing. This was my fault—I'd done this. I had to stop it somehow—stop Justin. But how could I without becoming his next target? I couldn't hear him say that name again, *Lamefield.* So I just stood there, paralyzed.

Ronald's face was a mask of terror. His eyes darted back and forth between me and Justin.

"So, do you sleep with Mr. Tummy every night, Ronnie boy?" Justin yelled. I heard a few snickers around us, and I glared at the crowd of people watching. How could they be so cruel to laugh at Ronald like that?

I leaned back against the lockers, feeling sick. *I was the one who'd started this*—who'd screamed out the secret I had sworn I wouldn't tell.

Out of the corner of my eye I could see Damon still standing there. He'd seen the whole thing and was probably more convinced than ever that I was Ronald's girlfriend, or a nutcase, or just the meanest girl at SVJH.

Blindly I broke into a run, heading for the safety of the girls' room and wishing I could run away forever.

I'd ruined Ronald's life and lost all hope of ever going out with Damon—all before first period.

Damon

I watched in shock as Jessica seemed to crumple back against her locker. Obviously she and Ronald were *not* a couple—that much was clear after everything I'd just seen. But they'd seemed to be friends at least. How could she yell out something so embarrassing about a friend and then just stand there while that bully Justin acted so harsh?

I zipped up my backpack and slung it over my shoulder, then headed off down the hallway, glancing at Jessica as I walked away. I almost stopped when I saw her expression. She looked miserable. I almost wanted to say something, anything, to make her smile. Why was *she* so unhappy anyway? Ronald was the one who'd been made a fool of in front of all those people, and Jessica was the one who'd started it.

Still, it didn't make sense. Jessica always seemed so nice—there was just something so . . . sweet about her.

It's not like I really know her that well, though, I realized.

I paused before rounding the corner, turning back one more time. Justin was picking on Ronald again and laughing really hard. Jessica just stood there beside Ronald, crumpled against the lockers.

Maybe I should try to help her, I thought. I didn't know what was actually going on between her and Ronald or Justin. But my instincts were usually right about people, and my instincts told me that Jessica was for real.

Just as I was about to walk over and say something, Jessica pushed her way around Justin and scrambled off in the other direction, her shoes clacking loudly on the floor as she ran.

I paused, wondering if maybe I should say something to help Ronald out. He'd practically climbed into his locker, trying to get away from Justin. But it isn't really the best thing to try to settle another guy's fights for him. That just makes him look even worse. And although Ronald looked like he was in pretty bad shape, I was sure Justin and his friends could make things even worse for him if they really wanted to.

I turned away and headed toward class.

Jessica is the one who should have said something,

Damon

I thought, shaking my head. But she'd basically abandoned Ronald, poor guy.

I'd always thought Jessica was different, special. It was time for me to accept the fact that I was wrong.

Bethel

Dear Diary,

It's weird the way people can surprise you, just take you completely off guard. When I first met Jessica, I knew exactly who she was—just another stupid wanna-be who'd do anything to be liked by the "right" people. Then she stood up to Lacey and stood by me. And I realized I had to stop being so sure of everyone. Because Jessica was okay. More than that. She was a real friend. So then I started to trust her a little. And I was sure that I could count on her. Then she betrayed me and went back to her fake friends.

See—you can't be sure of anyone, ever. Right?

Meet Your Candidates
By Charlie Roberts

The *Spectator* recently met separately with each of the candidates for eighth-grade class president to learn their positions on the issues. Here's how they answered our questions:

SPEC: Why would you make a good president?

BETHEL MCCOY: I'm a serious candidate who will look out for the interests of all the kids, even if they're not part of the popular crowd. If I'm elected president, I'll make sure *everyone* has a say.

KRISTIN SELTZER: Well, I think I'm pretty good at organizing things, and I have a lot of school spirit. I'm on the cheer squad, and I'd bring the same kind of enthusiasm to being president. If I'm in charge, I can get everyone to work together so we can plan some really cool dances and activities. I have a lot of *ideas*.

SPEC: The school board recently decided to consider uniforms for SVJH. What's your position on this issue?

BETHEL: I know a lot of people think uniforms are a terrible idea because they don't allow any individual expression. But what about the kids who can't afford the trendiest clothes? It's not fair to them to have to compete with the people who can. And we all know that in this school, if you don't dress the right way, you can't be popular. If we all wore uniforms, we'd have to see people for who they really are, not for the clothes they wear. So maybe we should at least consider it.

KRISTIN: Well, I really don't think it would be fair to force uniforms on us. People express themselves through personal style. We should have the right to dress how we want.

SPEC: What kinds of fund-raisers can we look forward to if you're in charge?

BETHEL: Maybe a five-kilometer race? And we could probably sell candy bars or wrapping paper. You know, stuff that everyone can do on their own if they want, not just big social events like the car washes and bake sales, where a lot of people feel like they don't fit in.

KRISTIN: Oh, the usual. Bake sales at the basketball games, maybe a car wash—things that are fun social events for everyone.

SPEC: How would you spend the money you raise?

BETHEL: Girls' sports teams need better uniforms and personal lockers and towels like the guys have. I think if the class had more money, we could finally reward all the great female athletes in our grade.

KRISTIN: It would be cool if we could get a band like Splendora at one of our dances. I think people would love that.

SPEC: Is there anything else you'd like to say to the voters?

BETHEL: Just that I'll work very hard if I'm elected.

KRISTIN: I'd like everyone to know that I'll make this the most fun year they've had so far!

Jessica

I approached Bethel's table in the cafeteria tentatively, hoping she'd finally be willing to listen to me. Yesterday she'd avoided me in class and at track practice. I mean, I understand that what she saw looked bad, but couldn't she at least let me explain?

"Hi," I said when I reached her. I hovered over the chair next to hers, watching her expression. "Do you mind if I sit here?" I asked.

She shrugged, and I plopped down in the seat, dropping my tray on the table.

We were both silent as I unwrapped my sandwich and took a sip of my soda.

"Did you forget your lunch?" Bethel asked, pointing at the soggy ham sandwich I'd picked up on the lunch line.

I nodded. "This looked better than their hamburgers," I explained. I glanced at Bethel's tray and saw a hamburger with one bite taken out of it, sitting on the side. I couldn't help but laugh.

Bethel frowned, but then she met my gaze and her lips started to turn up into a smile. Soon she was laughing too. "It was pretty bad," she admitted.

"Here," I offered, breaking my sandwich into two halves and handing her one. "I'm not that hungry anyway."

Bethel paused, then took it. "Thanks," she said quietly.

"No problem."

"So about yesterday—," Bethel began.

"I was just taping up one of Kristin's posters that was falling down, honest," I interrupted. "I would have done the same for you."

"I know," Bethel replied. "I was just so upset when I saw you there, but last night I kept thinking, and I knew that—I knew you wouldn't do that to me."

I grinned. "Good," I said, relieved. "Because if you didn't listen to me, I was going to kidnap you at practice today and make you listen. I was going to yell and scream and act crazy until you paid attention."

"You? Crazy? Never," Bethel teased. "Anyway, I know you're not taking sides with the campaigns, but I *do* still have your vote, right?" she asked, raising her eyebrows.

I swallowed, then opened my mouth to reassure

her when I heard a loud noise and a roar of laughter coming from the lunch line.

"What was *that?*" Bethel asked, sitting up in her seat and craning her neck to see. I gazed around her at the line, and my heart dropped instantly, like a stone tossed into a pond.

Ronald was at the front of the line, clutching his tray and looking kind of sick. Justin and Matt were right behind him. I couldn't see Justin's face that well, but I didn't have to.

"Those jerks," Bethel muttered, spinning back around. "What are they picking on Rheece for now?"

Ronald hesitated for a second, then started to walk across the cafeteria, heading straight toward the table where Bethel and I were sitting. I'd only had one bite of my sandwich, but I threw it onto my tray. I had this crazy fear that Ronald would try to sit with us, and I was ready to bail. Now was *not* the time to set things right with him.

"So what did you think of the *Spec* article?" Bethel asked. "Kristin came off sounding pretty superficial, don't you think? And her posters— they don't even *say* anything about what she'd actually do."

"Uh, I don't know," I said absently, focusing on Ronald as he got closer and closer. All my instincts as a runner had the adrenaline flowing through me, ready to bolt.

Jessica

Justin and Matt trailed behind Ronald, and as they approached, I could hear what Justin was saying. "What's the matter, Ronnie?" he whined in his annoying voice. "You look a little sick. Doesn't he look sick, Matt? I think he's missing his teddy bear. Ronnie gets so lonesome without Mr. Tummy." He poked Ronald in the side, and Ronald jumped, almost knocking the dishes on his tray onto the floor.

"Oops. Careful there," Matt said. "We wouldn't want you to drop anything." He stuck his foot in front of Ronald's, trying to trip him.

My breath caught in my throat. *Don't fall*, I thought. *Please don't fall.*

Ronald stumbled, then caught himself, but not before half his soup had splashed out of the bowl.

They were practically next to our table now. I looked down at my tray, hoping that if I avoided eye contact, Ronald would leave me alone. If he tried to sit with us, Justin would have a field day—*a Lamefield day*, I thought, cringing.

I listened as Ronald's clomping footsteps got louder and louder. Just when I knew he was right in front of me, I peeked up at him almost against my will, needing to see if he was okay.

Ronald stared right through me as if I weren't even there and walked by us.

I exhaled, suddenly realizing I'd been holding my breath.

"What was that all about?" Bethel asked, scrunching up her nose.

"Exactly what it looks like," I said bitterly. "Ronald Rheece being tortured by two creeps."

I watched over my shoulder as Ronald sat down at an empty table in the back of the cafeteria. I winced as Matt smacked the back of Ronald's head with the palm of his hand. Ronald's head jerked, but otherwise he didn't move. He just sat there perfectly still and silent, his back straight, until Justin and Matt walked away.

"That's disgusting," Bethel said. "Anyone who would enjoy doing that to another human being is a total waste of space."

"You're right," I said, my stomach twisting in guilt. I clasped my hands in my lap, pulling my arms in close to my body.

I didn't exactly feel like I deserved much space myself.

Kristin

"Do you think it would look better up here or over there?" I asked Brian, pointing at the two spots on the wall.

Brian stared at the poster in my hand, then up at the wall, and then back at me. "It'll look good either way," he said. He lifted his shoulders in a helpless shrug. "I'm just here for the carrying and reaching—don't ask me about how stuff looks."

I laughed. Brian had been great about my campaign, following me around patiently and helping me hang all my posters and flyers. He was even giving up his lunch period now to finish decorating the hallways while barely anyone was around. But every time I tried to ask his advice on something as simple as where to tape something, he got all shy. It was so cute—*he* was so cute.

"I think it should be higher, like above the lockers there," I decided. Brian gave a little nod, watching me with an intent expression. I felt my cheeks start to flush, and I quickly turned my back to him and stepped closer to the wall. I noticed a chair next to the bank of lockers and pulled it over, then climbed up on it and began to try and tape up the poster.

As I stretched up my hand, my sweater rose a couple of inches and I realized that some of my stomach was showing above where my jeans ended. I quickly pulled my arm back to my side, then tugged the sweater down with my free hand. I'm not superskinny, and I'm okay with that. But suddenly I felt all self-conscious about Brian seeing any part of me that he maybe wouldn't like. It was so weird being this nervous around Brian, my best friend!

"Need help?" Brian asked from behind me. "Aren't I supposed to be doing this part?"

I gulped, trying to get myself under control. It was *ridiculous* the way I was acting. Still, I just couldn't handle having Brian watch me right now. "Yeah, maybe you should," I answered, and I spun around to hop back down from the chair. Only somehow the move wasn't as graceful as I'd planned, and I started to stumble as I was getting down. I managed to clear the chair, but I could tell that all the wrong parts of me were about to land on the floor. Brian was instantly at my side. His hands closed around my waist as he saved me from the nasty spill, then he steadied me on my suddenly useless feet.

My breath caught and I stared up into his eyes, certain that if he let go, I'd crumple onto the floor in a second on my gelatin limbs.

"Are you okay?" Brian asked softly, gripping me slightly tighter as I started to sway a little.

"Uh-huh," I whispered. My heart was thumping so hard, I wondered if he could hear it. The hallway was completely empty, completely quiet.

Brian held me like that for a few seconds—it felt like forever—and then started to pull me toward him. He leaned his head closer, and a thrill of excitement raced through me at being so close to him. I let out a nervous giggle from all the tension in my body, then immediately my whole face heated up in embarrassment. But Brian didn't pull away—he started to smile instead, and another giggle escaped my mouth. Soon we were both laughing. Our faces were still so close that our noses rubbed together, and we laughed even harder. I stopped to catch my breath at the same moment that Brian grew quiet. Then, before I could even blink, he brushed his lips softly against mine in the sweetest kiss I could ever imagine.

Jessica

Dear Diary,

All I ever wanted was for Ronald to just leave me alone. I planned my mornings around avoiding him at our locker. I cringed every time I heard that loud, annoying voice call my name—or say anything at all to me. Then today I actually walked up to Ronald and said hi, just, you know, to be nice. Ronald turned his back to me and walked away—without one word! So, I should have been thrilled, right? Only I kind of got this stomachache right afterward. I'm sure it was just from the meat loaf at lunch, though. I forgot my lunch again today. I guess I've had a lot on my mind lately.

Damon

"So in conclusion," Kristin Seltzer announced brightly from the stage, "I'd just like to say that as your president, I promise to work magic for our class."

"You mean she's going to make the cafeteria food edible?" Brian joked quietly from his seat on my right.

I smiled back at him. Brian's running commentary was the only thing making this assembly bearable—it was really annoying how everyone at SVJH had to sit here and listen to all the speeches for every class. Why should I care about the eighth-grade president? I barely even cared who won the election for ninth-grade class president. But actually I had paid more attention to Kristin's speech since she and Brian are so close and Brian's a pretty good friend of mine. He'd been making the most jokes during her speech—probably because he was nervous for her, though I'm sure he wouldn't admit it.

"Or maybe she could make a couple of my teachers disappear?" Brian added.

I chuckled. But I stopped laughing the second Kristin stepped down from the podium and I heard a soft chant, "Rheece and Tummy," coming from a few rows behind us. I twisted my head around and saw—of course—Justin Campbell with his sidekick, Matt Springmeier. I quickly scanned the seats for Ronald and cringed when I saw him staring straight ahead, his mouth set in a grim line. Then I searched around for Jessica and found her sitting next to her twin sister, Elizabeth. She was slumped down in her seat, as if she were trying to sink all the way through it.

I'm not supposed to be staring at Jessica anymore, I told myself, forcing my gaze away. Not that it was ever my *job* to watch her or anything. But I'd kind of gotten into this pattern of keeping my eye on her, making sure she was okay. Now, though, after this whole mess she'd started for Ronald and the way she still hadn't tried to do anything to stop it . . . why should I be worried about her?

As soon as Bethel McCoy, the other eighth-grade candidate, climbed up onstage to give her speech, Matt and Justin quieted down. But soon after she began talking, they started in again. I couldn't believe it.

"Hey, I think Kristin really did make a few teachers disappear," Brian whispered. "How come no one's shutting those two up? I can't believe they're getting away with this."

"Maybe the teachers don't realize what they're doing," I said. Matt and Justin were talking just softly enough that the teachers, who were all sitting up front, probably couldn't understand exactly what they were saying. But still, they should have at least heard the noise if the rest of us could.

Bethel certainly knew what was going on—I could see it in her expression as she stumbled over her speech. "Excuse me," she finally said loudly, staring up at the back of the auditorium where Matt and Justin sat. "Could you guys please be quiet?" she demanded angrily. "I know exactly what you're saying, and it isn't funny. Could you do us all a favor and save the immaturity for later, when the rest of us don't have to listen?"

Our whole class went dead silent. Even the teachers didn't move or speak or make any attempt to get things under control. Bethel was handling it fine.

"You know," she continued in a more subdued tone, "one reason I'd really like to be class president is that I'm tired of the way a few people make life miserable for the rest of us. I want to speak up for every one of you, to hear what all of you have to say and take it seriously." Bethel paused and her eyes swept over the group. "That is, if you have anything *serious* to say," she added. "So, if what you want is respect and ambition for this class, then I hope you'll vote for me."

Everyone just sat there, still stunned, as Bethel stepped down from the podium. Then a few people started clapping. I joined in, and so did Brian, and soon everyone was applauding. It took guts for Bethel to say all of that in front of our whole class *and* the teachers. Unfortunately for her, though, I knew it takes more than guts to get elected.

Jessica

I sighed as I watched Ronald carefully removing all the books out of our locker on Tuesday afternoon. He kept his face turned completely away from me the whole time. It wasn't like I wanted Ronald to be my best friend or anything, but getting the silent treatment whenever I ran into him was starting to get frustrating. And the way Justin and Matt had acted in assembly today just made me sick—I knew then that I had to apologize to Ronald. I'd never meant to do this to him, and I understood what it was like, having the whole school laugh at you. Of course, trying to avoid getting back in *that* situation was exactly what had landed me in this one.

"Look, Ronald," I said to his back, "I'm . . . um . . ." I paused to glance around us and make sure no one was watching me. "I'm sorry," I finally muttered softly.

I waited for him to stop what he was doing, to look at me with one of his silly smiles and start chattering away, now that I'd gotten the whole stupid apology thing out of the way. But he barely even flinched at the sound of my voice.

"Can you stop ignoring me?" I asked, raising my voice a little and stepping closer to him. "I know what I did was terrible, but it was just an accident. I didn't mean to—"

"Hey, Rheece Geek, there you are!" Justin's voice bellowed. I froze, then slowly twisted my head in the direction of the nasal tone and saw Justin sauntering toward us. Why did his locker have to be in the same hallway as mine and Ronald's? Out of the corner of my eye I glimpsed an expression of pain come over Ronald's features.

Ronald immediately scrambled to get his books in his backpack, but he dropped a notebook and a bunch of papers flew out of it across the floor. He quickly started to scoop them all up and stuff them into the notebook. The Ronald I knew would never be that careless about his notes—he was obviously seriously freaked out.

"Hey, Ronnie, what's your hurry?" Justin asked as he reached us. "I brought you a present."

I edged away and managed to slip between two kids who'd stopped to see what was going on. I searched the hallway desperately, hoping to spot a teacher. Instead I saw Damon, arriving at his locker. He glanced at Ronald, a worried frown creasing his brow. I quickly stepped behind a tall guy next to me, hoping Damon wouldn't notice I was there.

"Look, Dork-o, gummy bears, just for you," Justin said, holding up a bag of candy. "I know you're into teddy bears, so I figured you'd like these." He laughed loudly, and a few other people snickered, but most just stared in silence.

Justin pulled a gummy bear out of the bag and dangled it right in Ronald's face. Ronald edged to one side, but Justin moved with him, waving the gummy bear about an inch from Ronald's nose. "C'mon, Ronnie. We all know how you love teddy bears."

Ronald turned away his head, his face flushing crimson.

"What's the matter, Ronnie? He's not your type?" Justin asked.

A bead of sweat trickled down the back of my neck as I watched in terror. If I tried to do something to help Ronald, Damon would see the whole thing. Justin would say I was defending my boyfriend—it would look like Ronald and I were a *couple*. But if I popped out now and just took off, he'd think I was a huge coward. All I could do was keep hiding where I was and pray that this whole disgusting scene would end quickly and Damon would leave without seeing me.

"You'd better let me go," Ronald said, trying unsuccessfully to dart around Justin. You'll be in big trouble."

I cringed, fully aware that he was just making this worse.

Justin burst out laughing. "Ooh, Nerdo's gonna tell on me," he said. "I'm so-o-o scared."

The tall guy I'd been hiding behind shook his head and then walked away, and a few others started to leave too. I shrank back against the lockers, and my eyes flickered around, checking out the people who remained. Some were just watching, as if it were a TV show or something. A few people stood in groups, whispering to one another. Only Damon actually seemed to care about Ronald—he was looking back and forth between Ronald and Justin, frowning in obvious concern.

Damon's gaze shifted to me. My heart sank as he caught my eye before I could look away. He stared at me with a strange expression of confusion that sent little shooting pains through my stomach. I quickly glanced away, mortified over what he must be thinking.

"Hey, what's going on here?" A deep male

voice boomed down the hall, scattering the kids who were left. It was Mr. Enrico, the biology teacher, striding toward his class, a cup of coffee in one hand.

Justin looked startled for about a tenth of a second, but then he coolly raised his hand and popped a gummy bear into his mouth, dropping the bag into his jacket pocket and striding off.

I glanced at Ronald for one last time before hurrying away. His eyes were really bright—in that scary way, as if he was about to cry.

It didn't matter that I'd lost my chance with Damon. I didn't deserve him anyway.

I didn't deserve anyone.

Kristin,

As usual algebra stinks, but at least Justin is providing some mild amusement with his gummy-bear antics. Yeah, it's a lame joke, but watching him beat it to death is actually pretty funny.

Only your buddy Jessica doesn't look too happy. She's watching with this face like she could strangle him. Maybe she's got a thing for Ronald, you know? They make a good pair.

Don't bother getting all mad at me, okay? Anything that makes algebra a little easier to take is worth it. Anyway, I know I said student government is lame, but do you need any last-minute help on your campaign? Not like it'll be tough to kick Bethel's butt. She's so uptight. But you know I'm here for you anyway.

Lacey

Lacey,

You know, sometimes your sense of humor totally escapes me. What Justin was doing is cruel—Jessica wasn't mad because she likes Ronald; she just doesn't want to see the guy tortured like that. I mean, what's Ronald ever done to Justin? That's exactly the sort of thing Bethel was talking about yesterday, and you know, I think she had a point.

Okay, okay, end of lecture. There is something you can do. Brian has a computer program that we've been using to design flyers that say Seltzer Sparkles. We can stick them in bags with some candy (not gummy bears!) and hand them out on election day.

Kristin

P.S. Can you believe Brian kissed me??!!

Bethel—Things to Do Tomorrow:

1. Hand out flyers in the morning before school
2. Vote!!!
3. Make sure no one sees me cry when I find out I lost
4. Ask my parents if I can go to boarding school

Jessica
Reasons to vote for Kristin:

1. She'd do all kinds of fun events.
2. She was the first person at SVJH who was really nice to me. Except for my sister.
3. She's going to win anyway.

Reasons to vote for Bethel:

1. She's never afraid to say what she thinks. She even made Justin and Matt look like idiots in front of everyone.
2. She was the second person at SVJH who was really nice to me. Except for Damon. Who is probably never going to talk to me again.
3. She won't lose as badly.

Kristin

"Hey, Josh," I said cheerfully as Josh Tyler walked by on his way to the school's front steps. I tossed him a bag of candy with my flyer inside. "Don't forget to vote today," I called out.

"Thanks," Josh said as he raised his arm to catch the bag. "You've got my vote," he added with a smile before heading up the stairs.

"Hey, guys," Brian yelled from next to me. I glanced over and saw some of his friends approaching. Brian grabbed two more bags from the box of candy sitting between us and pitched them at his friends. I smiled at him gratefully. Luckily I knew almost everyone in the eighth grade, but Brian knew a few of the kids who I didn't talk to much, and he'd been a big help.

Brian grinned back at me, and I felt a nervous giggle rise in my throat. This was crazy—Brian and I had known each other way too long for one kiss to turn me into a giggly mass of *girliness* around him. Okay, there was also the fact that he'd held my hand all the way to school this morning. Still, it was *Brian!*

"Do I get any free stuff?" a familiar voice asked teasingly.

I whipped my head around and saw Lacey striding toward me.

"Lace, I hope I don't need to convince *you* to vote for me," I joked. I reached down and pulled out a bag of candy for her. "But you can always stick the flyer up somewhere," I suggested as I handed her the bag.

She opened the plastic bag and took out the flyer, rolling her eyes as she unfolded it. "Sorry, but manual labor isn't my thing—even for you, Kristin."

I laughed. "But I've got your vote, right?" I pressed.

At that moment I caught sight of Bethel stalking in our direction, her face set in a familiar frown. I don't know what her problem with me is—I can deal with the fact that Jessica has two friends running for president, so why can't Bethel? She has a major attitude problem—those posters she hung up were *really* obnoxious.

Lacey sniffed. "Of course, but it's not like you'll even need it," she said loudly. I noticed that Bethel was almost right behind her now, and I shifted nervously, not in the mood for another scene like the one in Mrs. Adams's office.

"You know Bethel doesn't have a chance," Lacey continued breezily as Bethel continued to get closer. "You've already won," she finished confidently.

"Oh, really?" Bethel asked sharply. She stopped walking and stood next to Lacey, glaring at her angrily. "Last time I checked, the election wasn't over yet." She glanced down at the box of candy and flyers. "And if your friend thinks she needs to bribe people for their votes, doesn't that say something?" she asked, raising her eyebrows. Then she whirled around and jogged up the steps without a backward glance.

Lacey's eyes narrowed, and she clenched her fists in anger. "That girl is such a—"

"Lacey!" I interrupted, staring at her pleadingly.

Lacey's face cleared, and she smiled again. "Oh, well, it's not like she matters anyway," she said with a little dismissive wave of her hand.

I sighed. It's always so easy for Lacey to decide that people aren't worth her time. Although for once I actually agreed with her. I had no idea what Jessica liked about Bethel.

The next bus arrived, and I saw Jessica and Elizabeth get off. I waved them over.

"Hi, Jess. Hi, Liz," I said. "Have some candy." I held out two bags.

Elizabeth took hers, but Jessica hesitated, her eyes darting around anxiously. "I'd better not," she said.

Lacey snorted. "What, are you scared Bethel will beat you up or something?" she asked with a chuckle. "Don't worry," she added, stepping closer to me protectively. "Kristin's got *real* friends to support her."

Jessica winced, and I felt a stab of guilt. I'd never wanted to make her feel like this. None of this was her fault.

"Jessica is doing what she thinks is right," I explained. "Staying neutral."

"C'mon, Jess," Elizabeth said quickly, tugging on Jessica's sleeve. "Let's get inside." She looked over at me with a brief smile. "Good luck, Kristin," she said.

I forced a small smile. "Thanks," I replied.

As soon as they turned and started to walk away, I glared at Lacey. "Why did you have to do that?" I asked her.

She shrugged. "It's fun. And why are you defending someone who chose Bethel over you?"

I frowned, hating to admit that I'd kind of been wondering the same thing.

"Hey, I'm hungry. Can I have some of this candy?" Brian piped up.

I laughed, happy that he was there to break

the tension. Actually, I was just happy that Brian was there—anywhere—with *me*.

"Go ahead," I told him, smiling at Lacey.

"I'll see you later," she told me. "Good luck—even though you so don't need it." She leaned over to give me a quick hug, then turned and sauntered up the stairs, without even a glance in Brian's direction. Ever since I'd told her about me and Brian, she'd been kind of cold to him. Lacey can be kind of possessive of me sometimes, and I just hoped she'd get over it soon.

"Mmmm, Hershey's Kisses are the best," Brian said as he unwrapped one. He caught my eye. "Well, the second best," he said softly, blushing a little.

I bit my lip. "Thanks for all your help," I said. "You can, um—have as many kisses as you want."

He smiled, and his gorgeous green eyes lit up. Then he reached over and took my hand, lacing his fingers through mine. He squeezed gently, and I squeezed back.

Jessica

I entered the gym after lunch and joined the back of one of the lines for the voting booths. Keeping my gaze fixed on the shiny wood floor, I shuffled forward with the line, listening to the people chattering around me.

"You're voting for Kristin, right?" some girl in front of me asked her friend.

"Bethel actually had some good points," the friend answered, "but Kristin's so *nice*. And if she wins, it seems like we'll have lots of fun activities."

I held back a groan. Even some girl who wasn't friends with Bethel *or* Kristin couldn't decide what to do—so how could I?

I heard footsteps approaching from behind and turned to see who was heading for my line, hoping it wouldn't be Bethel or Kristin.

It wasn't—it was Damon.

Our eyes locked for a second, and then he changed direction, getting in the line next to mine instead.

He doesn't even want to stand near me! My

shoulders drooped as I looked back down at the ground, tracing the bright painted line marking half-court with my shoe. Damon was obviously disgusted with me—a guy as nice as he was would never have done what I did to Ronald.

"Hey, Jess!"

I glanced up again and saw Elizabeth running over to my side. When she reached me, she took a deep breath, then hoisted her backpack higher on her shoulder and flashed me a big smile.

"So, what are you going to do?" she whispered. "Who are you going to vote for?"

"I don't know." I moaned. I surveyed the people around us, making sure that either Bethel or Kristin wasn't lurking behind some tall basketball player or something. I'd become a paranoid wreck—always afraid of running into *someone*. First it was Ronald, then Justin and Matt, and now even my two best friends!

"You know, you could just not vote at all," Elizabeth suggested, raising her eyebrows.

"What?" I stared at her in confusion. "What do you mean—not vote?"

She sighed and moved closer to me. "I mean, if you can't decide and you don't want to feel like you took a side, it's not *required* to vote."

I paused to consider what she'd said, but my thoughts were interrupted by a familiar laugh from one of the voting booths. It was Justin's laugh, the one that I'd learned to fear more than the words *pop quiz*.

I leaned around the people in front of me to see what Justin was up to.

"There was no chance to do a write-in for Ronald and Tummy!" Justin said, stepping out from the voting booth at the head of Damon's line. He announced it so loudly that I could even hear over all the conversations around us. People started to get quiet anyway, staring in Justin's direction and trying to figure out what he was doing.

"Tum-my, Tum-my," Justin chanted, smiling at his own lame joke.

"What is his problem?" Elizabeth hissed. "He's not even funny."

I shrugged. "Maybe not, but he still gets attention."

Justin was moving through the crowds toward the exit, and everyone's eyes were on him.

I tried to shrink into myself as he got closer, hoping he wouldn't notice me.

"Jessica Lamefield!" Justin cried out when he reached me.

My stomach twisted. This was the third time he'd used that name around me in the past two weeks, but it was the first time he'd done it in front of so many people. This was it—my death.

"Where's your boyfriend?" Justin asked me.

"Where's Ronald Rheece and his teddy bear?"

"Ronald's not here," Elizabeth answered, stepping in front of me. "Now leave my sister alone."

"Uh-oh, Lamefield Squared is here—I guess I'd better leave," Justin said. He peered over Elizabeth and winked at me. "I'll catch you and Rheece Geek by the lockers later," he added before sauntering away.

"Are you okay?" Elizabeth asked me as soon as he was gone. The noise level around us rose again as everyone got back to their conversations.

"Yeah," I answered, even though I was anything but. I cast a glance at Damon, but his line was moving faster, so he was already way ahead. All I could see was the back of his head and his dark gray shirt. Still, it seemed like somehow even his *back* looked colder—like no part of him wanted anything to do with me.

I sighed and faced my sister. "I have to vote," I told her, remembering what she'd been saying before Justin's little show. "Staying out of things is exactly what's been messing up my life lately."

She shrugged. "At least the vote's a secret," she said. "So just do what your heart tells you to."

I nodded. My heart told me that whatever I did, one of my friends would be hurt, and I might lose *both* of them in the process.

If only hearts were like math teachers, I thought. *And always gave you one right answer.*

Bethel

It's not like I don't know what it's *gonna say*, I told myself as I approached the principal's office after school, where the election results were posted. Still, my heart was pounding furiously and little beads of sweat popped up on my palms as I got closer. I couldn't stop hoping that a miracle would happen—that I would win.

I wiped my hands on the sides of my jeans as I rounded the corner, then took a deep breath and walked into the office.

I blinked the second I stepped inside.

Kristin was the only one there, aside from Mrs. Adams. She whirled around when she heard the door open, and her face immediately scrunched into a sympathetic frown.

I gulped as my eyes started to fill with tears. I knew my answer now, for certain. But for some reason I wanted to see the words myself.

"I'm sorry," Kristin muttered.

I ignored her and strode quickly to the bulletin

board. I glanced up at the paper she'd been staring at when I came in and kept my face blank as I read the name next to Eighth-Grade Class President.

Kristin Seltzer.

"Listen, I know this was a tough race, but maybe now we can—"

"Don't bother," I said, interrupting her. I glared at her. "You don't care at all how I feel right now, and I know it."

Her mouth hung slightly open, and I felt a small flash of triumph.

Very small.

I lost the election.

I wasn't good enough.

I stalked off, wishing the annoying burning in my eyes would go away.

Jessica

I drummed my fingers on my desk, glancing at the phone as if it were a bomb about to explode at any second. Only, a bomb you actually *don't* want to explode.

Bethel had skipped track practice today. It was probably the first time she'd done that in her entire life, including the time when her ankle was hurt. That week she still showed up to stretch with us and cheer everyone on.

I'd known that being class president was important to her, but I guess I hadn't realized just how much losing would affect her. As soon as I got home, I called her house, but her mom said she couldn't come to the phone. It had been a couple of hours now, and she still hadn't called me back.

It doesn't look like she's going to, I told myself. I could at least try Kristin—things had been weird with us lately, kind of distant, but she wasn't *mad* or anything.

I took a deep breath and grabbed the receiver,

then punched in Kristin's number. It rang a couple of times before someone picked up.

"Hello, Kristin's house," a female voice answered.

I frowned, confused. It didn't sound like Kristin's mom, and Kristin doesn't have any sisters. Besides, who would say something like that anyway?

"Um . . . hello? Is Kristin there? This is Jessica Wakefield."

"*Jessica,* so kind of you to call," the voice answered coldly. And suddenly it clicked—I knew who that was—*Lacey.*

"Let me talk to Kristin," I said.

"Sorry, she's in the shower. But honestly, I'm not sure why she'd want to talk to you anyway. I mean, after you voted for *Bethel* today."

I swear my heart stopped right then, at least for a couple of milliseconds.

I thought the votes were secret! How did Lacey know?

I had decided to vote for Bethel once I was inside the voting booth because I knew she needed my help more than Kristin did and I wanted to stand by her. Plus I thought she'd make a pretty good president—she certainly did a good job telling off Justin and Matt.

"Could you just tell her I called?" I finally

managed to squeak. I couldn't show Lacey that she'd gotten to me—that was exactly what she wanted.

"Well, sure, but I wouldn't wait by the phone or anything." She laughed. "Kristin has plenty of people who care about her, Jessica. She has me and, of course, her new boyfriend, Brian."

My jaw dropped. Kristin and Brian were dating, and she hadn't told me? A wave of hurt washed over me.

"Oh, did Kristin not mention that to you?" Lacey asked. "I guess she figured you were too busy helping Bethel. It's an adorable story, the way he kissed her in the hall the other day."

I swallowed, fighting to keep myself steady.

"Please tell Kristin to call me later," I said, then hung up.

I sat back in my chair, feeling dizzy from everything whirling around in my head.

Lacey knew that I'd voted for Bethel somehow, and she'd definitely told Kristin, who must hate me. *Maybe Lacey doesn't actually know,* I reasoned. Lacey's like that—she'll say stuff to upset you, stuff she makes up, and then sometimes she gets lucky and what she says is the truth. I mean, how could she know who I voted for? It didn't make any sense.

But it doesn't matter, I thought miserably. Lacey

wouldn't make up the fact that Brian and Kristin kissed. And Kristin hadn't told me about that, which meant she was definitely upset with me either way.

I glanced over at my phone again. *Please ring,* I begged silently. If it didn't, then I'd have to face the fact that I'd lost my two best friends for good.

Kristin

"Did anyone call?" I asked Lacey as I stepped into my bedroom. I flipped my wet hair over my head and ran my fingers through it, inhaling the fresh flowery scent of my shampoo.

"Nope," Lacey answered.

Oh, well, it's not like Brian would suddenly start calling me all the time just because we were together now, right?

"Bored?" I asked her, smiling. She was sitting on the edge of my bed, her eyes kind of glazed over.

"Just thinking." She scooted over, making room for me. "Have you talked to your friend Jessica lately?"

I frowned. "Not much," I admitted. I tightened my robe around me and then plopped down next to her. "She's been so busy."

Lacey narrowed her eyes and pressed her lips together. "Busy hanging out with Bethel, you mean," she said.

I sighed. "Lace, you know how I hate it when

you start things with her. Jessica stayed *neutral* because she didn't want to hurt either of us."

"Neutral?" Lacey shook her head and folded her arms across her chest. "Kristin, she basically admitted to me when I talked to her earlier that she voted for Bethel."

A pang of hurt stung me, but then I remembered that this was coming from Lacey, not exactly the most reliable source. "You were talking to Jessica? Since when do you guys hang out?"

"We, uh, bumped into each other. But that's not the point anyway. What's important is that—"

"What's important is that Jessica's my friend," I interrupted. "And even if she voted for Bethel, it's not like I'd stop talking to her or something. That would be a *really* stupid reason not to be friends with someone." It was true, and as I said it, I realized that I probably should have done a better job of making sure Jessica knew that.

Lacey rolled her eyes. "You are way too nice sometimes," she said.

I grinned. "I didn't see you complaining when I let you copy my homework for the millionth time today," I teased.

"*Anyway*," Lacey jumped in. "Forget Jessica. I have to tell you about what Gel did this afternoon."

I smiled as she launched into her story, giggling at the way she described her high-school boyfriend, a guy she actually admits to staying with only because he has a car.

Lacey can be harsh, I know, but she's still my best friend, and I love her.

And Jessica's my friend too, I thought. *Isn't she?*

Jessica

I trudged listlessly toward my locker on Friday morning, no longer worrying about running into Ronald. I knew he wouldn't speak to me anyway. It was a growing trend—Bethel had never returned my call last night, and neither had Kristin.

I wasn't paying any attention to the people around me, and as I rounded the corner, staring down at my shoes, I walked right into someone.

I was about to mutter an apology when I glanced up and realized I was looking right into Bethel's deep brown eyes.

"Bethel!" I blurted out.

She stepped backward and smoothed down her clothes, casting me an annoyed glance. "Why don't you watch where you're going?" she asked.

I gasped at the coldness in her voice.

"I—I tried to call you last night," I said awkwardly, reaching down to straighten my sweater. "I wanted to make sure that you were, you know, okay."

"Right," Bethel responded briskly. "It's always good to find out which of your friends you can really count on."

I bit my lip at her harsh words.

"Bethel, I couldn't get in the middle. You know why—"

"I told you I needed your help more than Kristin did," Bethel interrupted.

"But I couldn't . . . ," I began again.

"You knew what this meant to me," Bethel argued.

I frowned, feeling anger begin to well up inside me. I'd tried so hard to be fair about the election, and now Bethel and Kristin both hated me. "I'm sorry you lost," I said, meeting her stare. "But it's not my fault that you did."

Bethel's hard expression faltered for a second. "Not *all* your fault," she admitted. "But maybe if you'd helped . . ." She trailed off.

"I explained this," I said softly. "You said you understood."

"I tried to," Bethel said with a shrug. "But I just can't get why you would choose *Kristin* over me."

"I didn't *choose* anyone!" I exclaimed. "That's the whole point—don't you get it? The only time I had to actually choose was when I voted. And then—" I stopped, realizing that my voice was rising very loud, like I'd taken lessons from Ronald or something.

"You voted for Kristin, right? Just like everyone else in our class."

I stared at Bethel, shaking my head. I couldn't believe how she was treating me.

"Maybe I should have," I said, then turned and hurried off down the hall.

How had everything gone so wrong, so fast? Just a couple of weeks ago Bethel and I had been close friends—almost best friends—and now she hated me.

Speaking of people who hate me, I thought as I got close to my locker and saw Ronald there. I took a deep breath and headed over, trying not to notice the way he inched in the other direction when I joined him.

We pulled out our books in silence, and I was just about to leave for class when Justin and Matt came striding toward us.

"Hey, Ronnie," Justin called. "Where's Mr. Tummy?"

Ronald just stood there, shoulders hunched, staring straight into the locker as though he was considering climbing inside and shutting the door.

Justin came up behind Ronald and poked his back. "How come you won't introduce us to your teddy bear?" he taunted.

Anger surged through me. I'd been fighting so hard not to be Jessica Lamefield again—to hold on to my reputation *and* to my friends. But whatever I ended up doing, things just kept getting worse anyway. Now I had no friends and nothing to lose.

I was sick of trying and sick of caring what happened next.

I stepped in between Ronald and Justin and stared right into Justin's eyes without flinching.

"Get a life, Campbell," I snapped. "No one thinks you're funny except for you and your idiot friend here." I nodded in Matt's direction.

Someone snickered, and Justin's smile drooped. He actually looked a little uncertain for a second. He recovered fast, though. "Well, isn't this sweet?" he sneered. "Ronnie's girlfriend is coming to his rescue."

I gulped, refusing to let the accusation stop me. "The only people I'm *rescuing* here are myself and everyone else in this hallway who has to listen to your stupid jokes," I replied.

A guy standing a few lockers down laughed, and Justin started to turn red. "Oh, really, *Lamefield?*" he said angrily, obviously struggling for a way to scare me silent.

But now that I'd stood up to Justin, I realized how easy it was to shut him up.

"Are you still using that?" I asked. "After this long, I'd think you could have come up with something new. But then again, it is *you*." I laughed, and I noticed some other kids nodding.

"C'mon, Justin, let's go," Matt said, taking a

couple of steps backward. "I don't have time for this."

"Whatever," Justin said, shrugging. He slouched away with Matt, obviously thwarted.

I felt a surge of pride as I realized that I'd done it—I'd gotten rid of Justin and Matt. I'd made them look like fools, just like they always did to everyone else!

I smiled at Ronald, waiting for his reaction. But all he did was stoop down and get the rest of his books together in silence.

Around us lockers clanged shut, and the hall gradually emptied out. I waited for Ronald to speak, to thank me for sticking up for him like that and risking my own reputation.

Finally Ronald zipped up his backpack and started to walk away.

I stared after him in surprise. "Ronald?" I said, confused.

He stopped and slowly turned around.

"Aren't you going to, uh, say anything?" I clutched my backpack to my chest.

"Why should I?" he asked coldly.

Hello?

"Because . . . well, because I got rid of them," I said.

"Yeah? So?"

My smile faded. I shifted nervously from one foot to the other, relieved that the hall was so empty. If anyone saw me practically begging for Ronald to thank me like this, they would definitely think we were a couple. Of course, Damon probably already did anyway, and he was the only one I really cared about.

"You think that makes everything better?" Ronald asked. "I'm supposed to be grateful now?" The bitterness in his voice took my breath away.

I opened my mouth to respond, but nothing came out.

Ronald gave a sharp laugh. "Thanks a lot, Jessica. You're a real pal."

"What's with everybody?" I exploded. "Did I miss the moment where I won the award for worst friend in the world or something?"

Ronald watched me calmly, unaffected by my outburst. "Jessica, none of this would be happening if you hadn't told everyone about Mr.—" He stopped and took a deep breath. "About the bear in the first place."

I leaned back against the lockers, gripping my books tightly to my chest. He was right—scaring away Matt and Justin didn't fix anything. I'd still betrayed Ronald. He shook his head, then turned and walked away.

I didn't deserve a thank-you. In fact, what I deserved was exactly what I'd gotten—nothing.

Damon

I hesitated for a second before stepping outside, groaning as I shifted my backpack around on my back. My Spanish textbook was really heavy, and I didn't need it for anything tonight. But then again, maybe I'd end up wanting to look up a word. You never know when you'll need to say *table* or *salad* in Spanish, right?

I sighed, then shoved open the door and took a deep breath of the fresh air.

It's not that I was *avoiding* my locker. I just hadn't really needed to go there much lately.

Right, I thought, shaking my head as I jogged down the front steps. *Carrying this heavy book home with me has* nothing *to do with not wanting to see Jessica Wakefield.*

Unfortunately I'm not very good at lying, especially to myself.

I slowed my pace when I caught sight of Justin Campbell standing in a circle with a bunch of other guys. They were laughing, which couldn't mean anything good.

I approached the group, then stopped a few feet away and peered around them to see what was going on.

"Give it back!" someone cried out from inside their cluster.

I cringed as I glimpsed Ronald Rheece leaping up to grab at a red jacket in Matt Springmeier's hands.

Instinctively I took another step forward to grab the jacket for Ronald, but I held myself back. As much as I wanted to help, Ronald had been teased way too much already to be "rescued" by me. It would just give Matt and Justin something else to tease him about.

The best thing I could do was stick around for a couple of minutes to make sure that no one actually tried to hurt the guy.

Jessica

There's only one good thing I can say *about this day,* I thought as I pushed open the door and blinked, trying to adjust to the sunlight. *It's over.*

I surveyed the couples sitting on the front steps. Some were holding hands; others had their arms around each other. I took a deep breath, then began weaving my way around all the lovebirds. When I reached the parking lot, I saw all the little clusters of friends hanging out and talking. Everyone seemed to have someone—except for me. I hadn't felt this alone since the beginning of school.

My heart skipped as my eyes landed on Damon, standing at the edge of one of the bigger clusters. He looked amazing, as always, in his black T-shirt and light blue jeans. He wasn't talking to anyone, but his gaze was fixed intently on whatever was going on inside the circle of kids, and he didn't look happy.

What was he watching anyway? It seemed

like they were throwing something around, something red. I squinted and raised my hand up to my forehead to get a better look. It was a red jacket, just like the one Ronald wears.

I moved closer to see what was going on, sucking in my breath as my whole chest tightened in dread.

The jacket flew out beyond the circle, and one guy leaped for it, suddenly giving me a clear view inside. Ronald was in the middle, arms above his head, desperately trying to get his jacket back.

My heart sank. There had to be five or six guys ganging up on him—and good old worthless Justin Campbell was the ringleader, probably hungry for revenge after what I'd done to him this morning. A familiar feeling of guilt crept over me as I realized that not only had I *not* helped Ronald, I'd probably made things worse for him by ticking Justin off.

"Want this, wuss?" Justin jeered, dangling the jacket just out of Ronald's reach. Ronald lunged for it, but Justin jerked it away. "I don't think so." Justin laughed. "I think I'm gonna take this home. Maybe draw a few teddy bears on it." He tossed it to a tall blond kid, Kevin somebody, I think, who threw it over to Matt.

"Hey, Ronnie, it's over here!" Matt taunted as

Ronald whipped around, trying to follow the jacket's movement. He still had on his backpack, and it swung heavily as he turned, throwing him off balance. He stumbled and almost fell, but managed to stay on his feet.

Justin laughed cruelly, and I winced.

I chewed on my lip, wondering what I could possibly do. If I stepped in, would it just get Ronald in more trouble?

I tried to remember why people had given up making fun of me, back at the beginning of the school year, when "Lamefield" was the joke of SVJH. It pretty much ended once I became friends with Kristin and Bethel. Even before that, I started hanging around my sister all the time, and that helped too.

So maybe if I act like it's really true about me and Ronald being a couple, they'll leave him alone. Guys like Justin only tease you if you're alone, if they think you have no friends to take your side. The only thing I could do for Ronald now was to march over there and show everyone that he's *not* alone. I knew this meant my chance with Damon would be lost for good—I'd be announcing right in front of him that Ronald and I were together—but worrying about that was what had gotten me into this in the first place. Besides, Damon had obviously given up on me already anyway.

Jessica

I took a deep breath and then, holding my head high, pushed my way through the circle. "Ronald!" I said loudly. "There you are! I've been looking all over for you! C'mon, we're going to be late!"

Matt stared at me, hesitating. I grabbed the jacket out of his hand and tossed it right to Ronald, who looked just as shocked. Then I took Ronald's hand—trying not to grimace from the way his sweaty palm felt against mine—and tugged him forward.

"We have a date at Vito's, remember?" I went on. "And I'm starving!"

Ronald stared at me with his mouth slightly open, but he didn't protest. I steered him away from the group of kids and down the sidewalk, keeping up a steady stream of loud chatter until we were half a block away.

Finally I shut my mouth when we were out of everyone's earshot and dropped Ronald's hand. "Once we get around the corner, you can take off," I said quietly, avoiding his gaze.

"What?" he asked. He stopped walking and looked at me questioningly. "Why would I want to?" he asked.

I stared back at him, kicking at the ground with my sneaker. "Because you hate me, right?" I asked nervously.

His face broke into a wide grin. "Jess, no one's ever . . . I mean, what you did just now—well, it was really nice. And after what I said this morning too. Why'd you do that for me?"

I shrugged. "You were right—that's all. I *wasn't* a very good friend." I stopped, feeling strange admitting to Ronald that I did actually care what happened to him. You know, just a little bit. "Anyway, I think if we just stick together for a couple of days, then they'll give up," I said.

"So, uh, we're going to Vito's now, right?" Ronald said, his face sort of glowing in that old way it used to around me.

"Um, well, I . . ." I imagined the scene at Vito's on a Friday afternoon. *Everyone* would be there. Could I actually go through with this?

Suspicion crept back into Ronald's face. He started to turn away from me. "I get it," he said. "This is just another joke, right?"

"No," I said hastily. "It's not. I just . . . I was just trying to think if I could actually go because I didn't really think about it before." *Who would be there?* I took a deep breath. "So, let's go," I said. "I really am starving."

Ronald's face lit up again. "Okay," he said, and we fell in step together, walking toward Vito's.

Ronald babbled all the way there, telling me some story about his math class that I think was

135

supposed to be funny. I only half listened. Really, what could possibly be funny about advanced calculus?

Can I fake a bad headache and bail? I wondered as last-minute panic settled in. *Change my hair really fast and pretend I'm Elizabeth?*

As Ronald pulled open the door to Vito's, something my mom always says popped into my head. *Taking responsibility for your actions builds character.*

Great. I was going to have a terrific character. And absolutely *no* social life.

Kristin

"Pizza's on me," Brian announced as he pushed open the door to Vito's.

I stopped and stared at him a little nervously. I didn't want him to think that being my boyfriend meant he always had to pay for me. Not that he'd actually said he was my boyfriend yet. But I was pretty sure that's what we were, boyfriend and girlfriend.

"Bri," I said quietly, "boyfriends don't always, you know, have to pay for everything."

I winced at the way the words came out and held my breath as I waited for him to respond.

An expression of bafflement came over his features. "That's not why," he answered. "It's 'cause you won the election."

I started to blush like crazy and looked down at the floor. Brian put his arm around my shoulders and pulled me against his side. "Can't a boyfriend buy his girlfriend pizza when he wants to congratulate her?" he whispered into my ear.

I glanced back at him with a laugh. "Definitely,"

I said, punching him lightly on the shoulder.

We strolled over to our usual booth, and I slid into the seat across from him, feeling like I could burst from happiness.

I leaned back as I tried to decide what toppings to get, then glanced over at the door when it opened.

Jessica and Ronald? That was strange. Maybe the two of them were getting to be better friends. Ronald did always seem really nice. I felt a pang of guilt as I remembered that I hadn't told Jessica yet about me and Brian. I'd been meaning to, but things had been pretty strange between us with the campaign and Bethel, and I'd figured it would be better to wait until the election was over.

That's now, I realized. It was definitely time I got things straightened out with Jessica.

I sat up straight and waved my arm around so she'd see me. "Hey, Jess," I called out. "Over here."

She caught my eye, and I smiled as widely as I could. She looked surprised and uncertain, so I started to motion again for her to come over and join us. I figured if Lacey had really talked to her yesterday, then she'd probably said something to make Jessica think I was mad. I had to let her know that wasn't true. Finally she returned my smile, then tugged Ronald's arm, pulling him with her over to our table.

I looked up at Brian. "It's okay if they sit with us, right?" I asked anxiously.

Brian shrugged. "Why not?" He smiled. "But I'm not paying for *their* food."

I laughed. "Not a problem," I assured him, turning to greet Jessica as she got to our table. Jessica stopped as she was about to sit down, and her eyes darted back and forth between me and Brian. I shot her a look that I hoped said, *I'll fill you in later,* and then scooted over to give her more room.

"Congratulations," she said as she settled in next to me. Ronald sat down on the other side of Brian, and the two of them started talking.

Jessica met my eye with a serious gaze. "I mean it," she added. "I'm sorry about . . . well, you know, about the way I've been all weird lately."

"Don't worry about it," I said. "It was a tough situation."

"So you're not mad?" Jessica asked. "Because when you didn't call me back last night—"

"Call you back?" I frowned. "I didn't know you called."

Jessica smirked. "I talked to Lacey," she explained. "I guess it was stupid of me to expect she'd give you the message."

I sighed. "No, she didn't tell me." I paused, shaking my head. "Look, Lacey said that you told her you voted for Bethel." Jessica opened her mouth to speak, but I cut her off. "I want you to know," I began, "that it's okay if you did. I didn't mean to make you feel like that, like I wouldn't be your friend or something if you didn't vote for me."

Jessica's cheeks flushed slightly, and she cast a quick glance across the table at Brian, then raised her eyebrows at me questioningly.

Ronald was loudly explaining some sort of scientific thing to Brian, and I figured neither of them was paying any attention to us.

"I wanted to tell you about Brian," I said *very* quietly, moving closer to Jessica so that she could hear me. "I just didn't want to make you feel any more pressured or caught in the middle than you already did."

"So it's true?" Jessica asked, her eyes lighting up with interest.

I let out a small giggle and nodded. "Why don't we make a bathroom trip?" I asked her.

She quickly stood up, and I slid across the booth and got up too.

"We'll be right back," I said to the guys.

I linked my arm through Jessica's, and we started walking.

"So, what happened?" Jessica whispered.

"Oh, Jess, he was *so* cute," I said as we wove our way through the tables to the rest room at the back of Vito's. I smiled at Jessica, eager to catch her up on everything and relieved that things were finally back to normal.

Bethel

I picked up the phone and dialed Jessica's number for the fourth time in the past ten minutes. I listened to about half of one ring, which was longer than I'd made it so far, and then quickly slammed down the receiver.

I'm not very good at saying I'm sorry.

I took a deep breath and dialed for the fifth time, gripping the phone tightly to my ear and resisting the urge to throw it across the room.

"Hello?" Jessica answered after two rings.

"Hi."

Silence.

"It's me, Bethel," I said.

"I know," Jessica replied.

I chewed on the ragged cuticle of my thumbnail, hating the uncomfortable silence that followed. It was clear that there was no way around those two, simple words.

"I called because I'm—because I shouldn't have gone off on you like that today." I owed her much more than that, after everything she'd

141

done for me and the way I'd treated her. "And I'm sorry," I forced out. Once I'd squeezed out the *s* word, the rest was easy.

"I went for a long run after I got home today," I explained, the words tumbling out of my mouth. "It kind of cleared out my head. It wasn't your fault I didn't win, and I don't blame you for not wanting to take sides. I mean, I am *not* a fan of Kristin's, but she's your friend. I guess I knew I wouldn't win, and I was just taking it out on you. I think I was so disappointed, I sort of needed a punching bag."

There was another short silence, and I held my breath.

"Okay," Jessica said at last. "But next time go do some kick boxing or something, okay? Being a punching bag is really uncool."

I let out a burst of air and laughed. "Next time I'll go for a run *before* I open my big mouth."

"Hey, why don't you come over tonight?" Jessica suggested. "We could rent a movie or bake brownies or something. Or I could paint all your nails bright purple and put some of those nail-art tattoos on them. That'll definitely cheer you up."

I laughed. "Sounds good. But not purple, okay?" I paused. "And Jess," I continued more softly, "thanks for voting for me. That was really nice."

Jessica was quiet for a second. "I didn't just do it as a favor, you know," she said. "I think you would do a great job. Really. I'm sorry it didn't work out."

"I'll be right over," I said, and hung up.

Knowing that Jessica was still my friend meant a lot. But knowing that she actually believed in me meant . . . everything.

Jessica

"Well, wish me luck," I said to Elizabeth as we climbed off the bus Monday morning. "Here goes a whole day of nerd-dom—the first of a week's worth."

"Wait," Elizabeth said, her face tightening in mock fear. "You forgot your pocket protector!"

I widened my eyes. "You know, you're right—maybe I should just abandon the entire plan now."

"Forget it." Elizabeth shook her head. "You were happier this weekend than you've been since the whole Ronald mess started. You're doing the right thing, standing by him."

I sighed and followed her into school, then said good-bye and headed toward my locker. I wasn't really as worried about hanging around Ronald as I pretended to be. Ever since I'd made up with Kristin and Bethel, not much could dampen my good mood. The only problem was when I let myself think about Damon Ross and how I'd totally messed up any chance I had with him. It seemed pretty obvious that after seeing me walk up and practically ask Ronald out, Damon would give up on me for good, if he hadn't already.

I shoved Damon out of my head, reminding myself that the plan was to *not* think about the guy.

I reached my locker, surprised that Ronald wasn't there yet. I worked the lock, then swung open the door. I was just about to toss a book onto the shelf when I noticed something there—one of Ronald's matchstick-construction thingies. I picked it up, smiling as I took in all the details of the castle. Then I glimpsed a folded piece of paper on the shelf below where the castle had been. I opened it and saw the words *Just a small thank-you* in Ronald's handwriting.

"You like it?"

I whirled around and saw Ronald smiling shyly at me.

"It's great," I said truthfully. "But you didn't have to do that. You must have spent all weekend on this."

"Well, I'd started it already," he admitted. "Actually, it was almost done. And I decided to give it to you because . . . well . . ." He stopped as his cheeks started to turn slightly pink.

"Thanks," I said, torn between wanting to be nice and not wanting to be, you know, *too* nice. After everything I'd been through, I didn't want Ronald to still think there was something up between us besides just being locker partners. And maybe . . . well, maybe friends too.

"Oh, did lover boy give you a little token of his affection?" Justin's voice mimicked from behind me.

I didn't even turn around. "Did you hear something?" I asked Ronald. "Sort of an annoying, squeaky sound?"

Ronald cocked his head. "I don't know. . . . Whatever it is, it's obviously nothing important."

I laughed. "Yeah, I think you're right," I said.

There was a pause, and then I heard Justin's footsteps disappear in the other direction.

I glanced around to make sure he was really gone and caught sight of Damon walking away from his locker. My pulse sped up as I watched him reach up and run a hand through his dark brown hair. Immediately I felt a stab of sadness. He'd probably seen the whole thing—which meant he saw me *not* denying that Ronald Rheece was my boyfriend.

Forget it, I reminded myself, trying to ignore the ache that settled around my heart. *He's a lost cause. Remember?*

Damon

Reasons to stop coming up with reasons and just ask Jessica Wakefield out:

1. I'm tired of making lists.

Jessica

I twirled the lock on my locker and popped open the door, then reached inside to take out my lunch. My hand froze when I caught sight of a red rose lying on the shelf next to my lunch bag.

I picked it up, carefully gripping a part of the stem without any thorns, and sniffed the flower gingerly. I smiled for a second as the beautiful scent overwhelmed me. Then I bit my lip, realizing that this was a very bad sign. Clearly I hadn't done a good enough job of making Ronald understand that we were *just* friends. I shut my eyes, inhaling deeply. I could at least pretend that the rose was from a real boyfriend, just for a second. . . .

"Where'd you get *that?*"

My eyes flew open, and I saw Ronald standing in front of me.

"You mean it's not from you?" I blurted out in surprise.

"Uh-uh. Sorry," Ronald said. He grabbed his lunch out of the locker while I just stared at the rose, stunned.

148

If Ronald hadn't put the rose there, then who did?

"Ronald," I said anxiously, "did you see anyone around our locker at all this morning? Did you, like, leave it open ever?"

Ronald frowned, his brow furrowing in concentration as he considered the question. "Actually," he finally said, "when I got back here from my calculus class, I was in a rush and I think I did leave it unlocked for a couple of minutes while I went to drop something off. But don't worry—I came right back, and I know I locked it then."

I pursed my lips as I realized that whoever had left the rose must have been watching us, waiting for a chance like that to leave the surprise on my shelf.

Don't think it, don't think it, I told myself, trying to squash the hope that was rising inside me. But Damon was the only person I knew whose locker was near mine and the only one I could imagine doing something so unbelievably sweet.

Yeah, maybe he'd do it for someone else, I thought sadly. *But why would he leave a rose for Ronald Rheece's girlfriend?*

"Well, I gotta go, so I'll see you later, okay, Jessica?" Ronald tossed some books onto his shelf and then hurried away.

"Sure," I said absently. I sniffed the rose again, carefully, as if somehow I could figure out who gave it to me from the scent.

Jessica

At least my first fear was wrong—Ronald seemed clear on where things stood between us. He'd given up the googly-eyed thing for the most part, and it barely fazed him that some other guy had left me a rose. Wait—I didn't even know if it was a guy. Maybe Elizabeth left it for me, or Bethel, or even Kristin since she was trying so hard to let me know that things were okay between us.

I sighed, then picked up my lunch and closed the locker, still holding the rose with my other hand.

I turned around and instantly almost dropped my lunch bag *and* the rose.

Damon was standing a few feet away, watching me with a small smile. He looked even more gorgeous than ever. As if that were possible.

He started walking toward me, and my legs began to shake.

"Do you like it?" he asked softly, gesturing at the rose.

Did I like it? Wasn't that something you ask when you're the one who gave the gift?

I gulped, then nodded. "It's beautiful," I whispered, my voice trembling.

His smile widened, and I was pretty sure I was about to pass out. I was totally lost in those amazing blue eyes of his, the ones that had been turning me into mush for weeks.

"I hope you don't mind that I, you know,

went in your locker like that," he said quietly. "Ronald left it open. But I didn't look at anything inside—promise."

My heart rate went off the scales. *It's definitely from Damon. The rose is from Damon. Damon Ross gave me a rose. Damon doesn't think I'm dating Ronald! Damon probably wants to—*

"So," he continued, interrupting my racing thoughts, "are you busy Friday night?"

"Friday?" I squeaked. "Friday night? No, no, I'm not—I am not doing anything. Nothing. Nope, not me. Not busy." I shook my head for emphasis, then quickly gazed around to see if any meteors were about to land next to us. This was closer than Damon had ever come to asking me out, and I couldn't shake the fear that something would pop up right as the words were about to come out of his mouth. But all I saw were kids walking by or getting stuff out of their lockers. "Why?" I asked, fixing my gaze back on Damon.

"I was just wondering . . . I mean . . . maybe you'd like to do something? Go to Vito's or just hang out?" His eyes stayed locked on mine.

A warm glow exploded in my chest, then spread through my entire body. I grinned up at him.

Of course, there was only one possible answer to *that* question.

Check out the **all-new**....

....(**Sweet Valley Web site—**)

www.sweetvalley.com

New Features

Cool Prizes

The **ONLY** official Web site!

Hot Links

....(And much more!)

You hate your **alarm clock.**

You hate your **clothes.**

You're going to love Jr. High.